W9-BSC-989

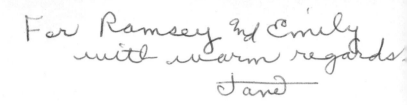

For Ramsey and Emily
with warm regards.
Jane

PETER FRANCISCO

—

VIRGINIA GIANT

Janet Shaffer

MOORE PUBLISHING COMPANY

DURHAM, NORTH CAROLINA 27705

Library of Congress Catalog Card Number: 76-025334

ISBN 0-87716-068-6

Dedicated to

Americans of All Ages Who

Care About Peter Francisco

ACKNOWLEDGMENTS

Recognition and appreciation are due the following who in either big or little ways helped me to produce a book which is, hopefully, worthy of its subject. This included assistance in critiquing, research photos, consultation, or publicity. Others, merely encouraged and gave the kind of support especially gratifying to those who try to originate something new, whether it be a book, a painting, a musical composition, or some other work requiring creativity.

All the members of my family
Epps Perrow, critic-friend
Lynchburg Public Library, especially Margaret Reid for invaluable help
Terry Bailey, Media Center, Lynchburg Public Schools, for special efforts
Michael Gleason, Albemarle-Charlottesville Bicentennial Commission
Joseph Rountree, Colonial Williamsburg Foundation
Ruth Cantor, New York literary agent
Lynchburg News-Advance
Charlottesville Daily Progress, Deborah Murdock and Bill Sublett
Brookneal Union Star, Herman Ginther
Lynchburg Magazine, John Lair
Lipscomb Library, Randolph-Macon Woman's College
Virginia Independence Bicentennial Commission, Park Rowse and
    Bettie J. Matthews
Lynchburg Bicentennial Commission
Hopewell Bicentennial Commission and Historic Hopewell Foundation
Sally and Alvin Gerhardt
Emilee Hines
E.L. ("Brag") Bragdon
State Department of Education, Mary Stuart Mason
Dr. Mervyn Williamson, English Dept., Randolph-Macon Woman's College
Lynchburg Historical Society, William Dunn and Robert Garbee
Faye Apple
Dr. Mary Williams, Randolph-Macon Woman's College Emerita
J. Quintus Massie, Society of the Descendants of Peter Francisco
Mrs. Bruce English, Society of the Descendants of Peter Francisco
Jones Memorial Library, Lynchburg
National Society, Daughters of the American Revolution
Campbell County Media Center
J. Paul Hudson, Jamestown Colonial National Historical Park
Don Walker and Frank Creasy
Carl and Cullen Rosen

FOREWORD

The childhood origin of Peter Francisco who grew up to become the Virginia Giant of Revolutionary War fame, remains one of the unsolved riddles of history. Despite speculation, research, and fanciful theories, the mysterious events which led up to his strange arrival in America still intrigue the imagination.

What is known is that in the year 1765 he was abandoned at the port town of City Point (now Hopewell), Virginia. He was thought to be about five years old at the time. Sailors in a longboat rowed him ashore from a merchant ship riding at anchor under a foreign flag.

The frightened young boy, dirty and ragged, was cast onto the nearly deserted dock, but it was obvious that his clothes were of good quality. Silver buckles on his shabby shoes were inscribed with the initials "P.F."

Dark-haired and dark-eyed, the boy looked Spanish or Portuguese. His language was a mixture of the two, combined with fragments of French. The only clues to his past were the silver buckles and the name "Pedro Francisco" which he repeated to the villagers who gradually flocked to the dock to stare at the bedraggled new arrival.

Pedro — or Peter — as the City Point townspeople called

him, became the ward of Judge Anthony Winston of Hunting Tower in Buckingham County. It was here he grew up to become a valiant hero in the colonial cause. He also made friends with many of the notables of his day. These included The Marquis de Lafayette, who became an American General, Nathanael Greene, the outstanding war officer from New England, famed orator Patrick Henry, Henry Clay, eminent statesman, and others. The orphan also made friends with people in many other classes and ranks — and probably a few enemies in the bargain.

A brief account of some of Peter's accomplishments during the Revolutionary War are outlined for history's sake. All are documented from material found in archives and other means of research.

Peter Francisco enlisted in December of 1776 as a private in the Virginia Tenth (later the Sixth) Company at the approximate age of 16. The unit, was commanded by Colonel Stevens who had taken over the command lately held by Captain Woodson. The Company joined the Continental army led by George Washington at a camp said to be near Middlebrook, Pennsylvania.

His great size undoubtedly helped earn him the title Virginia Giant, but his exploits in battle were those of an eighteenth century superman. His reputation as a swordsman and cavalryman began to grow after the Battle of Brandywine where he received the first of a series of wounds. It was during his recuperation that he formed a friendship with the young Lafayette which is said to have lasted a lifetime.

The Virginia Giant's most amazing exploits in combat were at the Battle of Guilford Courthouse located near the town of the same name in North Carolina. It was here he is credited with hewing down eleven British guardsmen. His weapon was a mighty five-foot sword given him as a gift by

Commander-in-Chief George Washington who had had it especially crafted to fit the soldier's size. In this battle Peter received his most serious wound of the war, but was miraculously saved by a benefactor and nursed back to health.

Additional battles in which Peter Francisco fought and performed with valor were Stony Point, Monmouth, Paulus Hook, Camden, Cowpens and others. After Guilford Court House he also served as a free-lance scout, routing out Tories and outwitting British guardsmen.

In addition to his prowess in battle, Peter Francisco earned a reputation for many of his fine human qualities. His sense of humor drove him to plan and execute practical jokes which have been told and retold until today they are legendary. Especially in Buckingham County, Virginia which claims him as a "native son." However, he lived in various other areas and counties in the state at various intervals during his long lifetime.

Peter's feats of strength rival those of the fictional Paul Bunyan. Some were performed during his war years, while others are recorded from annals when he was a private citizen. His Samson-like exhibitions of power sometimes helped others in situations where extraordinary strength were needed, but again, he may have been trying to appease his own strong sense of vanity.

Like all of us, he was a mixture of good and bad. Though he is a fine example of a self-taught, self-made man, he was sometimes immoderate and spent money foolishly. His liking for fancy clothes, fine horses and the life of a Virginia planter, led him into debt and his money worries were probably frequent. He was respected for his intelligence and attempts to develop his mind and social manners, but he may sometimes have lacked humility and good judgment. Though he is reputed to have been gentle and kind in most of his dealings with others, he is also credited with a violent temper when aroused.

Whatever his strengths and weaknesses, Peter Francisco deserves our admiration and gratitude for his contributions to the American cause. For the sake of interest among young readers, I have chosen to tell the story of his life in the form of fact-fiction, based on documented truth.

Most of the characters mentioned are real and are said to have played important parts in Peter's life. Recognizable names are those of Patrick Henry, Judge Anthony Winston (who was Henry's uncle), Edmund Randolph, Lafayette, Nathanael Greene, and many others you will recognize from your own past readings in history.

Others, such as Rufus and Samuel, the dock hands, Alex, Farmer Miller and similar characters interwoven throughout parts of the book, are fictional creations. His war comrades, John Aiken, Jim Billocks, Jed Londerlee and others will also be recognized as "made-up" characters necessary to the narration.

May the life of the colorful Virginia Giant and his achievements in war and peace capture your imagination as it has mine. Perhaps in this reading you may join with other Americans in recognizing and paying tribute to an orphan who became an American hero at a time in history when such men were much needed to defend the colonial cause. Without men like him, the story of our own history might well have had a different ending.

CONTENTS

Chapter

Francisco's portrait which hangs in the Governor's Mansion in Richmond, Va. is a copy of an 1828 portrait of Francisco by James Westfall Ford (signed) that is owned by the descendants of Francisco. (Virginia State Library)

PETER

FRANCISCO

MYSTERIOUS ABANDONMENT IN AMERICA

It was a calm early morning in June during the year 1765 when a ship from foreign waters anchored offshore near a James River harbor in the colony of Virginia.

The port was located at the town of City Point (known as Hopewell today) only twelve miles from Petersburg. Unlike the usual cargo vessel, it lay at anchor only a brief period, then set sail again to an unknown destination almost as swiftly as it had arrived.

But not before two sailors rowed ashore in a longboat to complete a strange and mysterious mission that piques the imagination of the curious to this day.

Except for two dock workers, the usually busy harbor was deserted that morning. Rufus, the taller and younger of the men, shaded his eyes with calloused hands, squinting across the olive green waters. He was anxious for the arrival of long overdue cargo ships and hoped this might be one of them.

Rufus leapt abruptly onto an upturned sea chest and stared harder.

"Look yonder,, Samuel!" he shouted. "A ship flying a foreign flag!"

"Aye, and a real beauty," Samuel agreed with a low whistle. "Don't rightly recognize its colors but she's a welcome sight."

The ship swept closer. When it was still distant from shore, the sailors aboard cast anchor and lowered a boat.

"Looks like a heavy bundle they're lifting into a dinghy," Rufus muttered. "We've a deep harbor. Strange they didn't sail closer to shore."

Samuel leveled his spy glass at the vessel. "The

longboats's heading straight this way."

"Who comes there? From what land hail you?" Rufus shouted.

There was no answer.

"Unfriendly lot," Samuel grumbled. "They look rough and mean. Especially the big one with the black beard. Be on guard."

As the boat pulled closer, the dockmen spied a small boy crouching in its stern.

"What goes here?" Rufus demanded. "Speak up, Sailors!"

Again no answer. Samuel reached for the knife concealed in his tunic. The boat idled alongside the dock. The swarthy-faced, bearded oarsman grasped the boy roughly. He heaved him onto the wharf, thrust a boot against a piling and the boat rocked to open water.

"Halt there! Halt, I say!" bellowed Rufus, shaking a fist at the sailors streaking toward their ship. "The King will have your heads for this!"

Samuel lifted the cowering boy to his feet. Tears and dirt smudged his already dusky skin. He was bewildered by their attempts at conversation.

All they could gather from his jumble of speech that sounded like Spanish or Portuguese with a mixture of French, was that his name was Pedro – or Peter Francisco.

Unbeknown to the dockmen, the abrupt appearance of the child on the City Point wharf had been observed by at least one other interested spectator. A traveler from Petersburg called James Durell, was riding toward the village in his shay when he saw the strange ship anchor, two sailors row a boy in a dinghy to shore, and drop him unceremoniously on the nearly deserted dock.

It is likely that James Durell joined the villagers who gathered at the dock later that morning (though this is not known). News traveled at a fast rate from person to person in those days, just as it does today, and word of a child abandoned at the nearby harbor created a flutter of excitement.

Many were sorely disappointed that they had not been witnesses to the early morning happening. The docking of ships from foreign ports invariably created excitement, but this one had sailed away before the town was properly astir.

Of course, one thing was certain, the boy himself was a curiosity. His sudden appearance and the mystery of the departed ship, were enough to keep tongues wagging for weeks, or longer.

The villagers tried not to stare too obviously at the forlorn boy in the tattered clothes. When several children snickered, a woman shushed them. "His clothes may be worn and dirty," she said softly, smiling at the boy, "but the lace of his shirt front and the velvet of his jacket and breeches are of the finest. Of course, he'll look better after a soak in a barrel of water and lye soap."

One of the smaller girls pointed to his worn shoes. "Look at the big buckles," she whispered. "They have fancy scratchings in the middle."

The silver buckles were engraved with the initials P.F., though there was little left of the uppers or soles.

"He's not ill-formed," one of the men said, eyeing the boy appraisingly. "I'll wager he's not more than five or six. But he's tall and strong for that age."

"Aye, he's that. And with those snapping black eyes and hair to match, he'd make a handsome lad if properly clad."

The crowd dissolved at mid-day. Rufus and Samuel gave Peter generous portions of their rations of bacon between slabs of corn bread and homemade spice cookies. Later he fished from the dock with one of Samuel's cane poles.

When he caught three sunfish he smiled for the first time. Already the strange events of the morning were beginning to lose importance and he began to relax in his new seaside surroundings. The terrible long sea voyage was over at last and the people in this new land seemed kind. He was young enough not to fear his uncertain future, or dwell too much on his past.

Except during the night. Rufus and Samuel arranged to have him sleep on a pallet in one of the warehouses bordering the wharf. Some nights, unable to drift off, he lay listening to the waves pounding against the pilings. When winds or storms churned the water with angry force, he was frightened. Again, he would sleep soundly, then awaken crying from ravelings of bad dreams.

It was at such times he remembered the nightmarish kidnapping, and the equally nightmarish sea voyage that followed.

One evening he and his sister, Angela, had been playing in the courtyard of their beautiful home in the land of his childhood. Their parents had been entertaining guests at a great fancy party and did not know what transpired.

Suddenly two masked strangers had crept from the shadows, grabbed first him, then his sister, and escaped with them through a pathway behind the garden wall.

Though he had kicked and scratched to free himself, it was of no use. Angela was luckier — or louder. While his own cries had been muffled by his abductor's rough hand, Angela's screams may have won her freedom.

The kidnappers had carried him to a waiting ship and the next day at dawn the long tempestuous sea voyage began. Besides being scared most of the time, he had been lonely and miserable from cold, and the food had been almost unpalatable. All of the sailors had been cold and mean and filled him with fear.

Except one. He had had yellow hair and a gentler face. More than once, his benefactor had taken his side and saved him from the vengeance of his shipmates. Without him, Peter was sure he would have been thrown overboard long before the end of the journey.

Especially after the wild storms at sea began. Once, enormous waves almost as high as the ship had swept over the top deck, and wind slit a sail. There had been other troubles too, making the sailors angrier and more mutinous daily.

In time they accused him of being a "bad omen," the cause of all their ill luck. After that they played sly cruel tricks, as though to take revenge, especially when the yellow haired man was not close by. Their harsh words had been equally as cruel.

Then the bright morning had come when the ship finally dropped anchor in sight of land. Inside he had felt happy for the first time in weeks. He had busied himself polishing the ship's brass, trying to keep out of the way, when the arguments between the crewmen and the captain raged back and forth. He was sure some of the angry words were about him. They had glared resentfully in his direction and the captain shouted orders he did not understand.

When strong hands grabbed him and carried him to the ship's ladder, he had expected the end. But instead he had been thrust onto the bottom of one of the ship's longboats, and was rowed swiftly ashore by two oarsmen.

Cowering, trembling in the bow, he had held his breath as the boat slowed, then anchored. One of the sailors had dumped him onto the dock as though he were a piece of worthless cargo, while the other steadied the craft. Then, without a word to him or to the two strangers on the wharf, they had rowed back to the big ship as though devils pursued the craft. Alone and orphaned, he had been left to make his own future in an unknown country without friends, decent clothes, or even a morsel of food for the 'morrow.

After a few nights, the dreams lessened, along with the frightening memories. He began to enjoy his new life at the harbor and his friendship with Rufus and Samuel. Sometimes he fished or waded in the shallow water at the shore. Again, he helped unload and stack cargo or worked at other jobs around the dock.

One day he went with Rufus to the long sheds called ropewalks where he watched workmen twist rope from the hemp that grew on surrounding farms in the county.

The hemp was first made into yarn, and then a "head" of hackled hemp was wrapped around the spinner's waist. A loose end was fastened to a hook-belt which led to the big "spinning wheel."

As the wheel was turned, the spinner moved backward down the ropewalk, controlling it from his waist. Then two or three skeins of yarn were formed into a strand and three or more were twisted into rope.

To be near water pleased him and seemed a familiar part of his past. He soon learned to recognize and name the smaller boats.

There were the rowing barges with awning covered seats in the stern, used by Southern planters for visiting and church-going. Then there were the "fall boats" for floating produce down the rivers from the back country. Clumsily and hastily made, they were often abandoned at the mouth of the river. Crude but sturdy dug-outs and river boats plowed the waters. But best of all to Peter were the big ships that docked in the harbor bringing cargo from other colonies or foreign lands.

Sometimes he tired of the river. Then he would play in the nearby meadows. Or Rufus would take him home to play with his two older boys.

"Let's play huzzlecap," said one of the boys one day. Peter was beginning to understand more words in English daily and was eager to play. "It's a game where you pitch pennies for fun. We'll show you."

Or sometimes they played stoolball. "You roll the ball at that three-legged stool over there called a cricket," explained the younger boy, Rolfe. "Claude here will defend the cricket goal. I'll go first and show you."

Too young to be really good at sports, Peter liked being with friends and learned to laugh and tease.

Some of the villagers took pity on him and sent food and clothes, especially Rufus Coiner's wife.

"Carry these breeches to that poor orphan," she would insist to her husband, or "Take these left-over vittles to that Pedro child. It takes a lot to fill up a young boy."

As the days passed, Peter's future began to concern many of the kindhearted people in City Point. A child of his years needed nurturing and a home, and certainly a warehouse was no place for a human to stay once cold weather set in for certain.

He was often the subject of conversation when they met in the village or visited each other back and forth in their homes.

"Most of us have children of our own to look after," said a local miller. "I for one can't take on another young one to raise and feed."

"And a strange foreign lad at that," added another. "My wife would have my head. She already complains at the work and worry of raising seven."

A bootmaker agreed, but had no solution. "He's not like our own children. Truth is, I can't rightly understand what he says, though my eldest tells me he's picking up the language quickly."

"He'll grow up a heathen if left to rough shoremen and the like," a member of the vestry predicted. "We'll all share the pangs of guilt."

"And be blamed for neglect," agreed another. "The boy's a weight and a worry."

Despite their concern, Peter stayed at City Point harbor an indefinite time. Some research indicates that he spent a part of that period in the Prince George Poor House. However, little is known of these first early weeks in America and the imagination is free to fill in the spaces.

PETER FINDS A HOME

One day in summer Peter's fortunes suddenly changed and the course of his life was set in a sure direction.

Judge Anthony Winston, a planter from Buckingham County, was returning from a trip to Williamsburg, the seat of Virginia's government at that time. He drove by the wharf for two important reasons.

The first was that he wanted to check on a long overdue shipment of English china he had ordered for his wife's birthday. The second was prompted by curiosity. He had heard the tale of the orphan boy abandoned at the wharf by sailors from a mystery ship, and he was eager to see him and make his own deductions about the boy's past.

Peter was fishing for perch among the pilings near the dock when the Judge strode to the water's edge. He was beginning to relax after his overland journey, and he breathed in the sea air with pleasure. It was good to leave the politics of Williamsburg behind, especially in these times when tempers were quick to erupt and it was difficult to know friends from enemies, patriots from loyalists.

He laid a friendly hand on Peter's shoulder. The boy glanced sideways, smiled, but went on fishing. The Judge baited an extra line and joined him.

Peter was glad to have a companion. He liked the

stranger's handsome clothes, kind face and quiet manner.

In turn Judge Winston was almost instantly attracted to the boy. As the day passed he began to debate an idea in his mind.

What would his wife say if he brought home a strange orphan boy to raise?

But did he want to take on an added responsibility? Would the boy be happy at Hunting Tower? He already had four children of his own to see after, and his wife might not take kindly to the care of another.

Still, there was much to do on his Buckingham County plantation. He had only recently left his land holdings in Hanover County behind to bring his family to this new county and an extra hand to help with field work and light chores around the house would not be amiss. Bound to him as an apprentice, he could provide the boy with the home he needed and an extra mouth to feed at Hunting Tower would be no hardship.

The Judge talked at length with Rufus and Samuel and the decision was made. As the ward of a prosperous Virginia planter, he would not only have a good home with proper food and clothing but certain other advantages.

After saying goodbye to his dockworker friends, Peter went willingly with his new guardian. They drove to Hunting Tower in an American shay with a collapsible top and a body suspended on bouncy hickory springs. At times it rattled over rock-bedded roads designed for use in wet weather. Again they skimmed so fast over sun-baked clay that Peter had to cling to the leather seat with both hands.

Judge Winston was welcomed warmly at his plantation home. Then, abruptly, he lifted the boy from the carriage into the midst of friendly smiling faces, white and black.

"And this is Peter, Peter Francisco. He's come to stay with us." The Judge quirked a questioning smile at his wife as he patted Peter gently on the shoulder. "That is, with Mistress Winston's leave. We have need of such a lad on the place."

Alice Winston glanced at his rough homespun cast-offs and then at the shabby shoes with silver buckles.

Peter bowed gracefully but at sight of her unsmiling face he was silent.

"Well, he'll need a thorough scrubbing and some decent garments, that's certain," she said. "And then we'll see."

That evening he rode on a brown and white pony as he and Judge Winston toured the plantation holdings. At bedtime Mistress Winston's face failed to soften and Peter was suddenly sad. Riding the pony had stirred childhood memories. He remembered another pony – one his father had given him for his fourth birthday.

Before falling asleep he cried for the lost parents and the little sister and older brothers he might never see again. He wondered if he would ever be happy at Hunting Tower. He dreamed again of the kidnapping, the miserable sea voyage, and the beautiful home he had once known among the mountains and the sea.

In time Peter learned to love plantation life. As he grew older he became an expert shot with Judge Winston's musket. He hunted wild turkeys, grouse, quail, rabbits, crows and wild pigeons. Sometimes he joined in hunts for larger game like deer, bear and the buffalo that roamed the deeply wooded forests of Buckingham.

On most summer mornings Peter was up at five o'clock or earlier to be ready for the day's work.

Tobacco was the main money crop. He helped sow the dust-fine seed in "new ground" in woodland seedbeds in early spring, and set out the seedlings in field rows in late May. Alongside other workers he helped harvest crops at the end of summer.

It was hard, tiresome labor, but there were free times when Peter could run off with his friends. Some of his favorite companions were sons of Negroes on the Winston plantation. Next to hunting, his favorite sport was fishing. The best spot of all was a secret cove on Willis River which he shared with Tony Debrell, one of his best buddies, the son of a plantation owner.

"I'll bet this is the best place to live in the whole world," Tony declared one day while they fished from a rock beside the river.

"Guess you're right, Tony," Peter answered. He had learned English quickly and now could talk intelligently with almost anyone.

"Only sometimes I'd like a little more excitement. Even danger. Things get pretty tame around home. My father had lots of narrow escapes and danger when he was a boy. He's told me some rousing tales about Indians."

"It'd be fun to go on an exploring trip to strange places and be a real hero in an adventure."

Tony laughed. "You're big enough for almost anything. I'll bet you could lick almost anyone in the county right now. You're only a year older than me, but you make me feel like a runt."

"My size does come in handy. I've been working at the forge lately. That's where to grow big muscles."

Black Alex, known and respected throughout the county for his skill, had been teaching Peter the blacksmith trade. He could make horse and oxshoes fit neatly, and his latches, hinges, andirons, spits, and nails were the finest.

Like most blacksmiths then he used charcoal for heating metal. Peter learned to blow the fire with a great bellows made from deerskins or a bull's hide. It kept him busy pumping to keep the fire hot and helping to smelt the bog-iron ore.

Black Alex was a friend as well as a teacher. "You're bound to make a fine smithy, Peter," he said one day. "Your arms and shoulders are built for strength. And you're quick, too. Someday you'll be the best blacksmith around."

"Thanks for your words. With such a good teacher I'm bound to learn the trade — and more besides."

LIFE AT HUNTING TOWER

One morning at breakfast Judge Winston shared some exciting news.

"Better step lively today. A letter from Patrick Henry says we can expect a visit either today or tomorrow, depending on the weather." The Judge smiled directly at Peter. "Knowing how much you admire my nephew and his views, I'm sure you'll help Mistress Winston with the chores."

"Will any of his children be along? Or other big people?" Peter asked. "I'll gladly give up my bed for company."

The Judge glanced slyly at Alice Winston. "There's a chance Parson Peter Muhlenberg from Dunmore County may drop in to discuss some political matters. He's a close friend of Patrick's and, for a man of the cloth, forward and fiery in his ideas." He chuckled and stroked his chin. "That nephew of mine is a very persuasive character, as we all know."

"I hope they stay a week — or at least a few days," Peter blurted out. "Company's exciting and keeps the days from getting dull or lonesome."

Mistress Winston eyed him with a mock frown. "They also make the victuals go faster, young man. And mark my words, before the week's out, there'll be others stopping by to chat with Mr. Henry. He draws people like flies to honey."

"No wonder," Judge Winston laughed. "Patrick has a voice like honey and he uses it as sweetening." He winked openly at Peter. "He also knows how to sting his victims — when he wills to."

Peter knew this for truth and reminded himself to be careful in words and actions.

"I wonder if he'll come in his shay or the family pleasure wagon," Mistress Winston pondered.

"Considering the chances of a rainy spell and muddy roads, he'd do best to travel from Scotchtown by wagon. Hanover County's a long way when the mud is axle deep and the streams are rampaging."

Peter could hardly wait for their visitor to arrive. Of all the outspoken patriots who came to discuss political matter with Judge Winston, Patrick Henry was his favorite by far.

Now that the Judge and John Nicholas had been elected as representatives from Buckingham County to the House of Burgesses in Williamsburg, Hunting Tower would attract more and more of the most brilliant, important men in Virginia. If he listened carefully he might hear stray bits of gossip and news that would help satisfy his curiosity about events outside Buckingham.

Britain's latest actions against the American colonies continually spiced conversations. Tempers flared and hot arguments resulted.

Most were word battles. Differences were quickly forgotten and friendships mended at the mention of card games or bowling or active sports. Peter was sometimes invited to join in fox hunts across country. Astride his mount, Starface, a gift from Judge Winston, he felt like a prince and was proud of his horsemanship. With practice he had learned to out-ride anyone near his age.

At swords it was the same. He had more patience to practice than most. His teacher was Jason Rupert, a frequent guest in the Winston home from Lunenburg.

"With your size and weight, you'll soon be a match for any foe in the South," Rupert said encouragingly one day as they feigned sword play in the Judge's study. "Handling a blade seems to come more natural to some than others."

"Who knows when the art of wielding the weapon may come in handy!" put in Peyton Randolph, a burgess and outspoken patriot. "The day's not far off when we'll all do well to practice the skill."

"May the Lord forbid," said a newcomer from Charlotte County. "Hardly a day passes that I and my good woman don't pray for peace in our land."

Patrick Henry had been listening from the chimney corner. He strode forward, stern-eyed.

"Would you have us abide the unfair taxes, Sir, that self-seeking ministers in London levy upon the colonies?" he challenged. "First, there was the sugar act and now the stamp act and more. No man should abide such villany without vigorous protest."

Peter was amazed at such eloquence. He had carried in refreshments for the guests, and loitered behind.

"It's tyranny!" shouted another patriot. "The Stamp Act demands that we affix stamps to all deeds, legal papers, newspapers and such. They cost a half-penny up to eighty shillings."

"And papers are illegal without them," agreed another. "This tax affects us all, rich and poor alike."

"It's wrong in principle," added Parson Muhlenberg. "Vestments or not, a man has to speak up for what he believes."

"The colonies are not even represented in the royal

Parliament," Patrick Henry continued. "Let's hope Ben Franklin, our representative in England, serves us well."

Just listening, Peter grew angry at the British leaders and wished he could speak out against them half so brilliantly and courageously. If only he could grow up faster he could help defend his new country against her enemies.

Tension increased daily. Hardly a week went by without stirring news in the *Virginia Gazette*. Luckily for Peter, Judge Winston liked to read aloud, and over the years kept him and the others in the family who listened, well informed on each new event in the colonies.

He learned about each fresh bout of opposition against the British as taxes were levied and kept in effect over a period of years. One of the most despised, the Stamp Act, which had been passed in 1765, had aroused such bitterness that it was finally repealed. But others took its place in time.

One of these, the Townshend Acts, gave reason for new and louder furor among the colonists. They imposed duties on such items as paper, glass, lead and tea which were shipped from Britain to America. Among other things, they provided salaries for judges and colonial officials, and granted rights to British officers to invade any man's home with blank search warrants.

Judge Winston kept Peter and the others informed about additional grievances included in the Acts, as well as other unfair laws that kept the colonists stirred up. One of the worst was that any Royal officer who committed a capital crime, even murder, would be sent to Britain for trial where he was certain to be acquitted.

Time passed and finally, the Townshend Acts were repealed — all except for the tax on that highly regarded commodity — tea.

Judge Winston's determination to resist British rulings was echoed throughout the colonies. He forbade its use in his household and many other citizens did the same. Shipments of tea were refused at ports in both the North and South and a riot broke out in Boston. English commissioners petitioned the Mother country for more soldiers and a larger naval force.

Peter could hardly control himself when he heard about the Boston Tea Party that came as an aftermath.

"The Judge says they've closed the port of Boston until the patriots pay for the 342 chests of tea they dumped into the harbor," Peter informed his friend, Tony Debrell. "I'll bet they'll refuse and I don't blame them."

Tony agreed. "There's the devil to pay. I've never seen people so angry. My own family too. They talk of little else."

Peter lowered his voice to a whisper. "I'm itching to fight back at those British. If it weren't for the Tories, I bet we'd be at war right now.'

He was not far wrong, for action was coming. The Virginia burgesses called a meeting in Williamsburg in May of 1774 to make plans. Many other states did likewise.

Judge Winston surprised Peter by inviting him to go along. It was a long trip and he would be glad for company. Besides, if the carriage got mired in the mud, Peter's powerful shoulders at the wheels would lift it clear.

He had never been so excited in his life. While the Judge attended long sessions with the burgesses, he roamed the streets, wandered in and out of shops, and sometimes talked with the craftsmen at their work.

His favorite walk was along the mile-long Duke of Gloucester Street. At one end loomed the capitol and the Governor's Palace set back from the street on the Palace

Green. He liked to dawdle long hours in the formal gardens among the boxwoods and flower gardens that put Mistress Winston's to shame.

When he could think of nothing else to do in the daytime he visited Bruton Parish Church and stepped softly among the weathered stones in the adjoining churchyard. Or, he would wander to the campus of William and Mary College with its stately buildings and watch the students as they walked to and from classes.

At night Judge Winston took him to Raleigh Tavern where the men gathered for sociability and more talk of politics. Peter found that he was happiest when around people and that he liked the tavern atmosphere with its light-hearted gaiety and air of celebration. He also discovered that money stayed a very short time in his tunic pocket and that he craved many of the things it could buy. Someday, he vowed to himself, he would return to Williamsburg wearing the fine clothes of a country gentleman and he would buy, not merely look at, the fine wares in all the fascinating shops.

Too soon it was time to leave the bustling town behind. He hated to leave the entertainment that was shared alike by whole families and by the lone hunters and backswoodsmen who found their way to Williamsburg for pleasure and business.

As they began the journey back to Buckingham, Peter could tell almost immediately that Judge Winston was more upset than he had ever seen him. His face was set in hard lines and he was impatient with the horses for no reason. He was silent until they reached the outskirts of town.

"Lord Dunmore's finally broken with the burgesses," he burst out. 'This time it's for good. Real trouble lies ahead, Boy."

Peter's quick temper exploded. He shook his fist at an

imaginary enemy. "The governor's a traitor and a simpleton. Who else can handle matters of government better than the burgesses?"

"According to Lord Dunmore the burgesses are foes of the King," the Judge admitted with bitterness. "He said more I'll not repeat. At any rate, after the chamber was dissolved, we met together and charted future action."

"And what might that be, Sir?" Peter inquired. "That is, if you're free to speak on the subject."

"There's no need for secrecy, Peter. The burgesses plan to run the affairs of the colony without royal decree. The time and place of our first independent meeting has not been set." Judge Winston sighed resignedly. "Difficulties and grave problems face the colonies, that much I know. There's no calculating where all these disruptions may end."

Peter clenched and unclenched his fists, almost without knowing it. He was ready for the future, whatever happened. If war came, he knew where his loyalties lay. At fourteen he was already a patriot, ready to fight and defend his adopted country.

PATRIOTS IN ACTION

The date of March 20, 1775 was set for the convention of burgesses. It was to be held at St. John's Church in Richmond. Williamsburg was no longer the gathering spot for the chamber since Lord Dunmore's latest action. It had become a hotbed of trouble and conflict.

"How would you like to go with me to the convention in Richmond, Peter?" Judge Winston asked one morning with a big smile. "You behaved well in Williamsburg and I'd welcome your company. Besides, in case of rain and bad roads or trouble with the carriage, you'd be of great help."

"I can't believe you mean it." He pumped the Judge's hand in a crushing handshake. "I'd like that better than anything else in the world, sir."

"It's a fine opportunity for you, Peter. You'll meet some of the most important and distinguished men in Virginia."

"Like George Washington and Thomas Jefferson? And of course, Patrick Henry?"

"Aye. Washington's probably already on his way. It'll take him as long as five days to get there from Mount Vernon. You've met William Christian from Fincastle And others like William Cabell and his brother from

Amherst. You'll meet other new faces as well."

From the moment of arrival, Peter was fascinated with the sights and sounds of Richmond.

"William Byrd the Second laid out the settlement around 1737," the Judge told him. "It was named for Richmond on the Thames in England."

' Does it really have stocks and whipping posts like Mistress Winston warned me?"

"You bet," Judge Winston laughed. "And they're much needed. Richmond's the county seat and every manner of mischief goes on."

Ships and boats of every description moved in and out of the waterfront harbor. Negroes chanted as they unloaded tobacco and other produce.

Leaving the roar of the falls behind, the carriage jolted upward over a long wooden bridge onto the cobblestone streets with their shops and taverns. Finally, they clambered up the hill to St. John's Church.

Peter wished he could write down the thoughts that spun in his mind as he wandered about the church yard and watched the delegates arrive. A few roughly clad men from the backwoods country arrived on horseback, but most were clad in their finest silk and satin breeches with bright waistcoats and boots.

A calm orderliness marked the early sessions of the assembly as the burgesses upheld the resolves of the First Continental Congress which had met in Philadelphia in September. Other matters of government were dealt with, and discussions led by Peyton Randolph, the presiding member, continued through the third day.

Peter was disappointed. He soon tired of the endless word battles and routine procedures. Secretly he hoped for excitement and drama to enliven the meeting.

On the fourth day he got his wish. Whisperings and secret sessions among the delegates emerged as the tension tightened and bitter arguments broke out during recess periods.

Finally the pressure was released after the Reverend Mr. Selden read aloud a prayer from the King of England. Debates followed. Tempers erupted. Most of the burgesses agreed that England had gone too far in taxing the colonies, but they had widely differing ideas on ways to retaliate.

Patrick Henry and other "Sons of Liberty" threatened armed action against Britain. Those with moderate views disagreed, bristling at the mention of violence as they proposed peaceful negotiations.

Peter's heart hammered. Patrick Henry jumped up to speak again and again. If only he had a quarter of Henry's eloquence! Or the courage to speak out so boldly!

When the orator presented a resolution to establish a regulated militia to provide strength and security for the colonies fierce arguments raged among the delegates. Henry motioned for silence. His face was sterner than Peter had ever seen it and his eyes snapped with a fiery light.

Voices dimmed as Henry began to speak again.

"Gentlemen may cry, peace, peace — but there is no peace. The war is actually begun! The next gale that sweeps from the north will bring to our ears the clash of resounding arms! Our brethren are already in the field! Why stand we here idle?" he demanded.

Henry brushed perspiration from his forehead. He studied his audience a moment, and when he spoke again his voice was softer.

"What is it that gentlemen wish? What would you have? Is life so dear, or peace so sweet, as to be purchased at the price of chains and slavery? Forbid it, Almighty God!"

He paused, stared like a man in a trance. Then he grasped an ivory letter opener from a nearby table, fingered its sharp tip.

Peter gripped his seat as Henry's voice rose to a shout.

"I know not what course others may take; but as for me. . . .give me liberty or give me death!"

As he exclaimed "Give me liberty. . ." he swept the letter opener upward, then let it sink slowly toward his breast at the word "death."

Peter was stunned and shocked like others in the audience. He clenched and unclenched his fists, then jumped to his feet to join the delegates stampeding around Henry. They clapped each other across the shoulders, shouting threats against England and defending the colonies.

Only a few stood apart in clusters. Their faces were set in firm agreement, but they were ignored by the enthusiastic majority.

Before the convention adjourned, plans were made for arming the colony. Patrick Henry was appointed chairman, assisted by Richard Henry Lee. Some of the other members were Andrew Lewis, William Christian and Thomas Jefferson.

Under a standing militia law (passed in 1738) each county was to form one or more volunteer companies of infantry and cavalry to be trained and ready for action. Each man was to be given a good rifle, if possible; otherwise, a common firelock. Frontiersmen could use tomahawks as arms.

In addition, Richard Carter Nicholas was made chairman of a committee, with Patrick Henry, to encourage arts and manufacturing in Virginia and delegates were chosen as representatives for the Second Continental Congress to meet in Philadelphia in May.

Peter was so stirred by Patrick Henry's speech that he wanted to join up immediately. He brought up the subject during the ride home to Buckingham.

Judge Winston opposed. "You're too impatient, Boy. I've told you about that before. And sometimes head-strong beyond your age. Remember, you're not quite fifteen yet. Wait a year or so until you're older and then I'll give you my blessing."

"But that might be too late. The war might be over before I even get to fight."

Judge Winston clucked to his horses impatiently. "There's little chance of that. The colony has scarce money for arms or provisions and there's no telling if we'll be able to raise an army strong enough to battle our opposition."

"That's why they need me! I'm big and strong and can fight as well as any grown man."

"That's true enough, but I'll have no arguing," the Judge said sternly. "Remember, you're still my ward, Peter, so that's the end of the matter."

Peter knew better than to oppose the Judge's word. He was obliged to obey until his day for action came.

PRELUDE TO ACTION

During the long period of waiting Peter occupied himself with tasks around the plantation and prepared himself for the day he would march off to war. His strength and endurance increased even more as he became an expert blacksmith under Black Alex's continued tutelage. He welcomed every chance to practice with sword or gun, either alone or with a friend, and in wrestling, no one near his age could offer any real competition.

As his reputation as a young Hercules grew, he was occasionally challenged by older, more experienced fighters. One hot June evening Peter sat drinking cider with friends at a crowded tavern table. Two thirsty farmers from Dillwyn staggered in. They were over-sized, sun-burned men, big muscled from field work, and after much mug-tipping were ready for a fight.

"Bet I could lick any man near my size and weight in this whole colony," bragged one called Spike.

"What about me?" said the other, named Charlie. "Course, I wouldn't want to tussle with such a good friend as you, Spike."

Holding their ale mugs aloft, the challengers hung their free arms around each other and shuffled toward the bartender, Horace.

"How about it, Horace? Got anybody here with the vigor to take on two champ scrappers?" Spike asked.

The barkeeper glanced toward Peter who was eyeing the braggarts.

"Got one but he's scarce old enough to fight two grown men. Lacks experience, too."

The farmers banged down their mugs and advanced on the bartender. "Let's see this young fella," Charlie demanded. "And what be his name?"

Scared, Horace backed off toward a far corner of the bar and gestured toward Peter.

"He's over there. Name's Francisco. Peter Francisco. But I don't want any kind of trouble. This is a respectable inn."

"You talk too much, Horace," sputtered Spike. "We don't figure on making any real trouble in your re-spec-table inn. Just looking for a little fun."

The two sidled toward Peter and went into action. Charlie yanked out his chair with a powerful thrust. As Peter crashed to the floor, the challengers attacked.

At first Peter was too surprised to move. Then he clambered to his feet and like an enraged bear, shook the farmers off his back. His eyes glittered and his face reddened with anger. He had not been looking for trouble, but now that he had been attacked, he'd not back down from a pair of bullies.

His big hands shot out. He grasped each man by the back of his shirt and wrenched them to their feet. Every eye in the tavern stared as he picked up a tormentor in each hand and cracked their heads together.

The half-drunk fighters crumpled to the floor, stunned. Almost immediately, Peter was sorry he'd been so rough. He stood by anxiously until the farmers revived.

"Guess we had that coming," Spike muttered, bewildered. "Francisco, you must be some kin of that Samson fellow in the Bible book."

"I'd as soon fight a wild he-bear," Charlie added, rubbing his aching head. "How did such a young feller learn to fight thataway?"

Peter laughed. "Practice, I guess. And I'll admit to a quick temper when someone comes at me. But I'm sorry I tore into you both so hard."

All three shook hands, then helped Horace close the tavern for the night. Peter had made two loyal friends and enhanced his reputation for strength and skill among the citizens in the county.

Meanwhile, such patriot leaders as Patrick Henry and others, were worried. And for good reason. Too few volunteers were willing to gather for drills in preparation for joining the colonial army. They were critical also of all the lukewarm colonists, men and women of all ages, who didn't seem to care if retaliation against the British was forthcoming.

"Plenty of our citizens talk about independence from Britain," Judge Winston grumbled during a conversation at Hunting Tower, "but not enough to fight for it. We need more grown men itching to get into battle like you, Peter."

"You're right," agreed Obadiah Woodson of Prince Edward County. "Big talk and little action. A mere handful offer their services from each town and village."

"We've too many Loyalists to Britain and not enough staunch patriots to do the fighting," said another.

"Only cowards fail to take up the gun or sword," Peter exclaimed. "I wish I could go off to battle tomorrow."

"Your waiting time is almost up, Peter," Judge Winston sighed. "And I'm bound to my promise to let you join up. Just a few more months and I'll give you my blessing."

"Have you decided what unit you'll join when the big day comes, Peter?" Edmund Randolph asked.

"The Tenth Virginia Regiment, sir. I'll sign as a private

in the infantry."

"I'm sure you'll help make it one of the best," Randolph predicted as he said farewell.

Peter was determined to do just that. At sixteen he is said to have weighed approximately 280 pounds and measured at least six feet six inches tall. His patriotic fervor ran high. No lukewarm sentiments for him, or unconcern about the fate of the American colonies and British tyranny! He was more than ready to fight for what he believed and for the rightness of the colonial cause.

CAMP LIFE AND BRANDYWINE

Peter never forgot his first months in camp following his enlistment in December, 1776.

He was uncomfortable much of the time and lonely, even in the midst of a growing band of army recruits. Impatient by nature, the suspense of waiting for action vexed him and he had everything to learn about field life.

True to his word, he had joined the Tenth Virginia Company (later the Sixth) as a private, serving under Colonel Stevens who had taken over the command lately held by Captain Tarlton Woodson. In time the regiment moved across country to join the Continental army led by George Washington at a camp said to be near Middlebrook, Pennsylvania.

Troopers who had fought with the Commander-in-Chief during the long 1777 winter in Morristown, New Jersey, and in other campaigns, were pessimistic. Howe, the British general, might strike anywhere, anytime along the Atlantic coast. According to late reports he had packed his 15,000 men into a fleet of 260 ships and headed out to sea. Philadelphia, only 50 miles away, was a likely target for attack.

Tension heightened. The men were almost afraid to sleep at night. Their only relief from boredom and the strain of waiting was to talk endlessly among themselves over their situation.

"Howe's a sly one," muttered John Aiken from Prince Edward County, a veteran who walked with a permanent limp from frost bite that bitter winter. "I hear he was spotted heading full steam up the Chesapeake. That could mean action's close — or it could be another false rumor."

Peter had been too unsure of himself to speak out in group pow wows until now, but he was beginning to feel a part of the unit. He glanced up from cleaning his rifle.

"Howe's tricky all right. He's keeping General Washington and a good part of the other leaders guessing."

"I've been wondering when the young giant from the South would get up the nerve to join in," Jed Londerlee from North Carolina remarked. "If I were a Britisher, I'd look out when the fighting gets started and they turn you loose."

"How much do you weigh and measure, Francisco?" John Aiken asked. "Can't rightly guess your age, but I'd say at least sixteen, judging by my own boy at home."

Peter pinked with embarrassment. He was proud of his size and strength, but self-conscious about his age. "It's anybody's guess," he drawled quietly, then grinned at the friendly faces around him. "We grow 'em big in Buckingham County."

"Must take a heap of grub to fill up that hollow from top to bottom," John remarked.

"Hollow is right," Peter agreed. "I've been hungry ever since I joined up. I guess I never appreciated home cooking before."

"You've likely been spoiled like the rest of us," added Robert Hill from Amherst County. "I can still taste those good home-cooked dinners like fried chicken and yams and other vittles. Army eating's the same day after day, what there is of it."

"I can stand the food and heat and the pesky insects," put in Mack Turner from Petersburg. He was a much respected veteran who had helped storm the Hessian garrison at Trenton. "But what aggravates me is that nothing's happening. What we need is a chance to move and a little excitement."

A few days later the arrival of a foreign volunteer from France provided them temporary excitement. He was the subject of conversations throughout camp. The recruit's full name was Marie Joseph Paul Yves Roch Gilbert du Motier, Marquis de Lafayette. He had been given the rank of major general, though he was less than twenty years old and had never fought a battle.

Some of the soldiers were jealous, others resentful.

"He's probably just another adventurer out for high rank and pay while we plain foot soldiers do the hard fighting," Jed Londerlee commented. "Still, I have to admit that some of the foreigners help our cause."

"A blue-blooded Frenchman like this Lafayette should have stayed at home," quipped another. "I hear he left a beautiful young wife behind to fight with our forces. He must have selfish motives of his own."

Mack Turner came to the Marquis's defense. "Maybe he's a square one. As I heard it, he had to slip out of his own country secretly and he sailed over in his own private ship called the Victory. Could be this Frenchie will help lead us to victory."

Mostly Peter kept his thoughts to himself. He hoped he would have the chance to meet the foreign volunteer sometime, and was impressed by his unselfish action. It took courage for a man to leave his own country to fight for another.

General Howe continued his maddening reluctance to rush into battle. Routine rifle and sword practice and maneuvers took a part of each day, along with calvary drills for those lucky enough to have horses. Peter had brought along his beloved Strawberry, a white mare Judge Winston had given him at the time of his enlistment.

Restlessness among the men intensified until finally on August 22, 1777 Howe's great fleet emerged from the ocean mists. The British army landed at the head of Chesapeake Bay, only 50 miles away from Philadelphia.

Now, at last, Washington ordered the march forward to meet the enemy. After recuperating from the long, wearisome sea journey, Howe and his troops drove north. The colonials were to halt the British as they advanced slowly on Philadelphia.

On September 11, 1777 Peter engaged in his first major conflict at a quiet flowing stream south of Philadelphia called Brandywine Creek.

The Americans were outfought early in the battle. Like Peter, many were new recruits and at the first onslaught by British troopers, they lost courage and retreated. Some streaked to the surrounding forests on foot, while others spurred their horses across open fields to safety.

Peter stood his ground. The explosion of guns and cannons stiffened his determination to revenge the enemy, and when he saw a comrade fall, his anger drove him to fight harder and without fear.

Gunfire intensified. From behind tree trunks, across the water. On the narrow beach skimming Brandywine Creek. Mack Turner was beside him during much of the fighting. They had become good friends, and when a shell grazed the burly linesman on the temple, Peter lifted him over his shoulder without concern for danger and carried him to a point where the wounded were being treated.

When John Aiken fell soon after from a gun shot in his middle, Peter felt tears rise. Old John had told him about his children and breeding Spanish horses and the farm he hoped to go back to.

He carried his second friend to a sheltered spot near a

makeshift hospital and took time to bathe his face with water from his canteen. Suddenly he felt nauseated from the acrid smoke of gunpowder and the pain everywhere around him. War was hard, not valorous and noble as he had dreamed of it as a boy at Hunting Tower. It was easy now to understand why both new and veteran fighters panicked and fled from battle, sometimes refusing to re-enlist at the end of their leaves.

Peter saw the foreigner, Lafayette, cantering beside Washington to take command at a weak and dangerous point of battle. They both looked resplendent in their handsome military uniforms. He wished fleetingly that he and Strawberry, by some miracle, were riding beside them.

Strawberry was grazing in a cluster of birches to the right of the battlefield. There had been little chance to use her in close combat, but now orders from "Joe Gourd" Weedon, leader of a Virginia brigade, brought her into action.

Peter's division and General Nathanael Green's sharpshooters swept to Sullivan's aid across four miles of rugged territory. Almost immediately they plunged into battle at a wooded pass near the peaceful Birmingham meeting house.

Again Peter stood staunch alongside seasoned veterans and the braver of the new enlisted men. They battled toe-to-toe, musket-to-musket. The young giant's gentleness and usual good humor had given way to fury. He was learning that his explosions of temper in battle drove him to impulsive action that made him a soldier to be feared.

Fresh British troops swept forward suddenly from an unexpected direction. Their target was the exhausted remains of the Virginia unit which had held ground. The defenders battled with desperate force without hope of victory.

Peter's movements had become almost automatic. Flashing and thrusting as in sword drill, he remembered the familiar routines as though in a half-forgotten dream. He had been de-horsed from Strawberry! And he was out of ammunition for his musket.

"Draw swords!"

"Slope swords!"

He and the enemy moved until the tips of their weapons were about three inches apart.

"On guard!"

"Cut and parry, one!"

The real battle between opponents began.

"Recover!"

"Cut and parry, two!"

When the dizziness started, Peter thought it was from exhaustion. Then he felt a sharp hurt in his arm and he swayed, staggered. If only the strange sound in his ears would go away. . . .

He remembered outsparring his enemy before he sprawled headlong on the battlefield, felled by a stray shot, his first wound in what was to be a long and heartbreaking war.

LAFAYETTE, CONVALESCENCE
AND NEW BATTLES

Peter came to hours later in a temporary soldiers hospital back of the lines. He was amazed to find himself being treated as a hero, with the special consideration usually reserved for wounded officers.

More than once he was commended for his outstanding bravery and daring at Brandywine. He relished the praise as he began to recover from battle fatigue and as the infection from his wound gradually lessened. Special credit was given to others among the unit of staunch Virginia troopers who had stood firm against Cornwallis. Though many fell and the battle had ended in defeat, they had helped save the American army from complete disaster.

Over and over in his mind Peter retraced the events of the battle. He thought of John Aiken and Mack Turner, special friends who had been killed or wounded, and of his beautiful horse, Strawberry. During the confusion of the fight she may have been shot, stolen, or wandered off across the countryside. Like John and Mack, he might never see her again.

The first night following the battle, Peter had stayed with the army at Chester, Pennsylvania. His wound had been dressed by one of the army surgeons, then the next day he and others with less severe wounds, had been taken by water to quarters in Philadelphia.

British troopers moved closer and closer to the capital city. Escape to safer territory was the only hope for the suffering remnants of the army about to be trapped within.

Peter was moved overland to a peaceful Moravian community at Bethlehem, Pennsylvania, fifty miles north of the city. It was a religious refuge established by Austrian and German Puritans on the banks of the Lehigh River. He was put in the care of a family named Beckel who had turned part of their home into a hospital for the convalescing soldiers. With nursing care and kindness he gradually recovered from his ordeal. It was in the Beckel home that he met and formed a deep friendship with a man who was to influence his future.

They met one afternoon soon after Peter's arrival. He was grateful for the simple room with its cot, a trunk for belongings, and a table with a shaving mirror.

Mr. Beckel, a stocky farmer in plain clothes, brought his evening meal.

"My good wife has brewed some soup that will set you back on your feet. You've had a bad infection and need building up." He tiptoed to the door of the adjoining room and peeked in. "The same goes for the officer across the hall."

Peter was instantly curious to know the officer's identity. And why was he, a private, quartered next door?

By noon of the next day his fever had cooled and he could walk unsteadily. He shuffled to the hallway for exercise and was about to return to his room when he heard a voice call out cheerfully.

"Is that you Madam Beckel? If not, come in anyway, whoever you are," the voice invited. "Push open the door and come in."

Peter did so hesitatingly. He stared at the orderly inside the door and then at the face on the pillow. Somehow it looked familiar. . . .

The room began to spin. He grasped the door frame to keep from falling. The orderly steadied him and led him to an unoccupied cot in the room.

The bedridden man tried to raise up from his pillow,

despite his elevated, thickly-bandaged leg. He waved his aide aside.

"Louie, why not take some air while this young soldier recovers his strength and we become acquainted." He turned eagerly toward Peter. "I've heard about your heroic fighting at Brandywine. In fact, I saw one exploit with my own eyes." He relaxed, arranged his pillows more comfortably. "It was a chance of fate that we were sent to Bethlehem. The Old Sun Inn is overcrowded with wounded. We're fortunate that religious folk like the Beckels are taking in the overflow."

"Yes, sir. They are fine people," Peter managed to say.

"I am Gilbert Lafayette and I'm delighted to meet you and to have a companion in suffering. I understand musket balls got both of us. Which injury is worse — an arm or a leg — I can't say. At any rate, I'm glad I was able to get you in here where you'll get well at a swifter pace. Men like you are needed back in the lines."

Peter was tongue-tied. No wonder the wounded man's face had looked familiar. He had watched the French recruit take the field at Brandywine alongside George Washington. He felt shy in his presence, but the Marquis was a ready conversationalist. His French accent was confusing at first, but he was quick to repeat words or explain their meaning.

"The Virginians who held ground in your unit are heroes," said Lafayette. "Such courage and determination. You helped save the American army."

Warmed by the Frenchman's praise, Peter relaxed. "But what's happening with the war, sir? Is our side holding firm?"

The Marquis smiled, shook his head. "No sirs, please, Peter. At least not behind these doors. We're equals, though not in rank. The friendship of two soldiers is not the business of others. I'd like you to call me Gilbert."

He frowned suddenly. "And now to answer your question. General Washington was defeated at Brandywine and Philadelphia is doomed. I'm told that Howe is advancing on the city."

"But that's where the Congress has been holding its sessions. It's the seat of government!"

"Just between us, I've learned that the Congress had fled to Lancaster, Pennsylvania and there's talk they may have to move again, to York. It may become the temporary capital. Philadelphia will be in British hands within the week."

Through visits from friends of the Marquis and some of Peter's recuperating comrades, the two soldiers continued to keep in touch with the war. Inquiries about John Aiken and Mack Turner brought welcome news. Both were in hospitals recovering from their wounds. As for Strawberry. . .there was no way of knowing her fate. . . .

The two men listened to gloomy accounts of the near massacre of "Mad" Anthony Wayne's troopers at their camp in Paoli during a surprise night attack by the English. They also heard criticism of George Washington and his conduct of the war. Both defended him as a wise and courageous commander who was often misunderstood.

While Peter and the Marquis were recuperating, their friendship as well as their bodies had time to knit. Peter told his new confidante about the Winstons, Patrick Henry, his boyhood at Hunting Tower, and even about his abandonment at the City Point dock and the terrible voyage by sea. He still remembered the kindness of the one sailor who had defended him against the others when they accused him of bringing bad luck when their ship almost floundered during a typhoon. Other details of the kidnapping and his past were refreshed by telling them to

Lafayette, but they were depressing at the same time.

The Marquis was intrigued. "I'd like to see that mystery cleared up," he said with deep concern. "Maybe some day when all the fighting is over, you'll manage to somehow solve the riddle."

"I hope so," Peter answered fervently. "Nobody can guess how lost I feel sometimes. It's like being an orphan, even though I'm not."

"I'll wager there's some splendid royal blood flowing in your veins. You look and act the part. I'm certain you come of no peasant stock."

Peter was pleased. His friendship with Lafayette brightened the otherwise boring days. He had almost forgotten the misery of battle and was ready to return to the front where officers were desperately trying to fill their ranks.

Howe had marched into Philadelphia on September 26. Many of the remaining Americans in the city claimed loyalty to the King and Parliament.

"I wish we could get out of here soon," Peter said to the Marquis one morning. "The British have a camp nearby at Germantown, and our own troops aren't far away. If it weren't for the doctor vowing I'm not ready to fight yet, I'd be out of here tomorrow."

Lafayette surveyed his still-bandaged, elevated leg ruefully. "And I would be with you except that I can't walk. The wound was a bad one, I'm told." He smiled at his restless friend. "But there's no holding you here for long, no matter how much I'll miss you. We'll figure out a way for you to get back in action."

That October Peter returned to the American lines at Germantown with the help of a farmer patriot and a stout wagon. He was just in time to join in a strategic maneuver near Germantown, Pennsylvania, north of Philadelphia where Howe had stationed his main force of less than nine thousand. Washington's troops stretched out for seven miles west to east covering four roads which converged as they passed the town. The plan was to march four columns of Americans, led by John Sullivan, Nathanael Greene, John Armstrong and William Smallwood on each of the roads during the night, hitting the British at dawn at four points simultaneously.

Unfortunately, a heavy fog swept in following a drop in temperature, disrupting the timing of the well-planned move. Peter stumbled forward with his comrades, bewildered as they, sometimes lost in the enfolding mist that grew denser toward morning.

Despite confusion and error on the part of some of the American leaders, Greene's main force broke the British line at one point and smashed into the town with close fighting.

"We've won a small victory at least," Peter gloated to Mack Turner beside him. Mack had recovered from his wound at Brandywine and was back in action. "We've taken the redcoats by surprise, even with the fog and blundering."

"It's about time we turn tables after all the defeats for the Continentals. Let's give 'em a hail of shot and listen for the yells."

The victory was a brief one. Cornwallis marched reinforcements from Philadelphia and confusion spread among the Americans. Howe ordered his remaining troops to reform in the yard of a square stone mansion that loomed out of the mist. It was owned by a Tory, Judge Benjamin Chew, who opened his doors to the retreating English soldiers. They turned the house into a temporary fortress, shooting from every opening and putting the Americans to flight.

Suddenly it was all over. Washington could do nothing to stop the retreat on every side, and what had looked at first like victory was turned to defeat, with 1,000 casualties and 400 captured.

Peter's wounded arm hurt from the exertion and he was weary and discouraged. He almost wished himself back with Lafayette at the Moravian retreat, but now it was too late. His decision to return to the lines had been made in haste and there was no turning back.

Peter's next military assignment was on Mud Island near the New Jersey coast. Men stationed at Mercer and Mifflin, two American-held forts, were ordered to prevent British ships from passing up the river with war supplies. Howe could not occupy Philadelphia for long without sufficient cargo. Bombardment and daily attack on the forts intensified, with the result that channel-sweeping guns and other American defense artillery were gradually destroyed.

Fort Mercer at Red Bank had been attacked, forcibly, but the colonials had made a successful stand. Peter was part of the garrison of 450 men stationed at the Mud Island fort which now came under heavy fire.

His ears roared from the explosion of mortars and other big guns. The barracks and the protective palisades surrounding the fort were blasted, leaving no defense. Replacements rowed over from the New Jersey shore after nightfall, but so many had been wounded or killed that there was a tragic shortage of defenders. The cold November weather worsened, food was short, and the men's morale slipped lower daily.

"Frigates and ships-of-the-line are moving up the channel," a look-out guard shouted one day. "Find cover. They're out to take the fort!"

"We'll set fire to the ruins first," yelled another. "The redcoated devils will find nothing but rubble and ashes for their trouble."

Peter was among the survivors of the five day assault after which they managed to escape and rejoin Nathanael Greene. His growing confidence in his ability to fight and survive had been boosted by battle and he felt ready to withstand almost any hardship which might occur.

They heard two bits of cheering news while awaiting the next action. One was that the Continental Congress which had reassembled in York after Howe advanced on Philadelphia, had adopted the Articles of Confederation as a way to unite and govern the thirteen states until the war was over. After that the members of Congress went home leaving Washington's army on its own.

The other good news was about the war which had been raging in New York.

"Huzza! A victory at last!" Peter exclaimed when he heard about General Burgoyne's surrender at Saratoga. "It's about time the redcoats learned to take us Americans more seriously."

" 'Ole Burgoyne and his officer friends figured they were going to split the colonies into two parts and bring us to our knees," agreed another. "For once their plans failed. This calls for a celebration."

There was very little to celebrate with. The men were hungry most of the time and there was always a serious scarcity of other supplies. Peter spent part of one day patching his battered boots, and he had learned to sew his ragged clothes together. Soldiers and officers alike grumbled about the bungling of the inefficient quartermaster unit, but as the war went on shortages grew worse instead of better.

The injustices the soldiers complained about were very real. During the early years of the war no official uniforms for enlisted men had been issued. Men such as Peter who came from rural districts were obliged to wear their own farm clothes, usually homespuns. Frontiersmen had no choice but to wear their rugged buckskins even on the hottest summer days. A few state regiments like the Delawares and the Marylanders had regular uniforms and equipment. Finally, late in 1778 a shipment of uniforms arrived from France. The coats were brown and blue with red facings. For the first time a large segment of the army came close to having official uniforms.

However, the uniforms came too late for the soldiers who faced the ordeal of Valley Forge that winter. In November Washington ordered the army to winter-in at quarters near the Schuylkill River twenty odd miles from Philadelphia. For the newer recruits suffering would become an almost unbearable ordeal. For other toughened veterans like Peter, it would intensify and test a hard-won endurance.

VALLEY FORGE AND SURVIVAL

Peter and his comrade, John Aiken, who like Mack Turner had returned to combat after his wound at Brandywine, shivered as they poked the all-night fire they were tending. Both had rejoiced at rediscovering each other at Valley Forge. Peter had feared that he might never see his friend again after carrying him from the battlefield.

"We're almost out of grub again," John complained. "A man can do without blankets if he must, or even shoes and a proper uniform." He sighed, clutched at his mid-region. "But when a soldier's stomach's been without decent food for more than three days, it's time to look on High for help."

Peter had been standing guard since nightfall. Like many others, his feet were wrapped in rags to stave off frostbite. Still, he was better off than some. What remained of his clothes at least covered his body, while some in his company wore only breech-cloths in the bitter weather.

"I used to complain about the army vittles the cooks dished up," he replied to John Aiken. "But I'd settle for more of the same right now." He sidled closer to the fire. "At least we've chinked our log hut to shut out the worst of the winter wind."

"But what's the good if we've nothing to stoke our bodies from within," John grumbled. "Congress and the bungling quartermaster unit are responsible for food and supplies being held up all along the line. It's scandalous."

A relief guardsman, Jim Billocks, joined them at the campside. He was miserable from a body itch that had spread through camp. So far, Peter and John had escaped the pestilence, but it could strike at any time. Men died daily from more serious maladies, and others suffered deeply from the cold that left many with bleeding feet and frostbite that plagued them the entire winter.

"I'd give my next ration of rice or Indian meal for a hunk of soap. Then I'd melt some snow and heat a bucket of good hot water to soak my feet in," Jim said with a wistful smile. "If I could shake this pesky itch and get a belly full of food once in awhile, I figure I can make it through the winter."

"I'm told that some farmers won't sell their food to the colonial army," put in John bitterly. "But they will to the British for English gold that pays for their comforts while soldiers freeze and starve. There's no fairness in that."

As the winter stormed on, there was even more reason for complaints among the men. A German, Baron von Steuben, arrived in camp to command the drills and maneuvers which he claimed would whip what remained of the scare-crow army into top fighting shape.

Ignoring the snows that crusted the plateaus of Valley Forge, the men were forced to drill daily despite their suffering. He maintained iron discipline and routine, resorting to flares of temper when the men performed badly.

At first Peter and most of the men resented the Baron and his dictatorial methods. But slowly, as he drilled and re-drilled the squads, platoons, companies, regiments and entire divisions — something happened. The men found they could move smoothly together. Peter's attitude toward the foreigner changed and he took pride in his ability to follow orders quickly and correctly.

"He's a nasty Prussian all right," admitted Jim Billocks,

"but I'll agree he knows his business. Finally I can do a right-face and left-face without tripping over my own two feet. And when we're out there marching so smoothly together, I almost forget my cold feet and empty belly."

Dan McCormich, a mountain man from Southwest Virginia, disagreed. "I never forget. That von Steuben has too much temper and gall for my blood. He acts like he's God Almighty keeping us out there in the snow and ice, sometimes from sunrise almost to sunset."

"Aye. And he calls a man down for next to nothing," added Jim Billocks. "How would it go if we had such a bossy billy goat as top general in place of Washington?"

"I saw the Baron light into you the other day," Peter said, grinning. "For a minute I thought you were going to break rank and give him a good poke."

"I almost did, but held my temper in time. There's talk against General Washington for appointing him as drillmaster. And we've all heard of the other nasty talk about Washington as well. It angers me no end."

"John here told me there's even a plot on to make General Gates the commander-in-chief," Peter put in grimly. "Folks criticize Washington for mistakes and faults that aren't of his making. As for me, I'm with the General!"

Most of the men felt the same way, as did the Marquis de Lafayette who spent part of the winter at Valley Forge and was one of Washington's main defenders. Lafayette had been assigned by Congress to take command of a proposed army to invade Canada, but recruiting efforts had failed.

Lafayette had returned to Valley Forge that winter of 1778. At scattered moments he and Peter held long conversations over past and present events. They were jubilant when the plot against Washington failed and the lies against him were proven to be part of a jealous conspiracy among high officials.

Peter survived the winter better than most. He had grown taller and thinner, but the drilling by the Baron had toughened all of the men who survived. His hands were chapped and sore, but his strength was needed for such daily chores as carrying great vats of water from a creek over a mile distant.

During idle moments his thoughts drifted to the past. He remembered details of his life at Hunting Tower, and once in awhile he tortured himself with memories of the kidnapping and sea voyage which he could never forget.

Sometimes, especially during the desperately cold nights when sleep was broken with misery, depression gripped him. Would he ever learn the truth about his childhood and all the strange circumstances that had brought him to America?

But more important now — would he live to see the end of the war? When would the suffering stop and when, oh when, would peace come again to his adopted homeland?

TWICE WOUNDED

March came. Then April. Valley Forge greened and life flowed again. The men were wildly elated at the news that France had joined forces with the Americans. A strong ally could bring the war to a swifter, perhaps victorious end.

The British leaders grew increasingly uneasy. With reinforcements from the French army and navy on the way to aid the stubborn rebels, action would escalate. Perhaps too fast. Sir Henry Clinton, who had taken over Howe's command in Philadelphia, was ordered to evacuate and move to New York. He decided to shuttle his troops across the Delaware into New Jersey, and thence to his destination.

Washington was still at his Valley Forge headquarters in Pennsylvania. Repeatedly he consulted with his officers before deciding on a counter move. Finally, they evolved a plan whereby the army would cross the Delaware to South Jersey in pursuit of Clinton who was handicapped by a cumbersome train of 1500 wagons.

It was June and the weather was torrid. Rain streamed in sheets, making roads almost impassible and the camps miserable with muggy dampness. Then, alternately, came baking suns, burning the men until they were irritable and complained bitterly at the interminable marching.

Peter was impatient at the slow pace, but the British were even slower, sometimes advancing only six miles a day. The colonial militia destroyed bridges wherever possible. Clinton's troops had to rebuild each one before their wagon trains could cross safely.

Finally, when they reached hilly country, Washington

decided to attack.

Peter was jubilant when he heard that Lafayette was to lead the offensive. Washington had felt obligated to ask Major General Charles Lee, second in command, to lead the attack, but at first Lee had refused the offer.

Then he changed his mind. He was impressed that Lafayette would have a force of 6,000 men under his command, so he reclaimed his rightful leadership, snatching it from the Frenchman. His vacillation only added to his reputation for weakness and aroused fresh contempt. Few soldiers respected him as a leader, but they had no choice but to obey his orders. The rumble of the British wagon train already sounded in the distance and action was close.

The army overtook Clinton near Monmouth Courthouse in New Jersey. Temperatures shot toward 100 degrees. Lee had neglected to issue instructions to his brigadiers the previous night, and as a result chaotic confusion swept through the ranks.

When they struck arms, the brigades advanced in no order or line of battle. Despite sharp fighting by some units, others retreated almost immediately, either from panic, heat sickness, or disgust with Lee, who refused to order a strong stand against Clinton.

Peter glimpsed Commander-in-Chief Washington galloping up a side road from Englishtown. His face was florid with anger.

"What is the meaning of all this, sir?" he demanded.

"Sir? Sir?" asked Lee in amazement.

"I desire to know the meaning of this disorder and confusion."

Washington, who usually kept his emotions under control, then unleashed his fury. He roared at Lee, ordering him to the rear, while he took over the command.

Scott's Virginians joined Wayne s faltering troops in

firing steady volleys against the British. They fell back to a stronger position.

Cannons and muskets exchanged endless fire during the humid heat of battle. Sunstroke increased casualties on both sides. Peter imprinted details of the battle scene in his memory. Washington on his handsome white horse riding fearlessly up and down the lines, encouraging the men. Soldiers cheered as he cantered by. Peter among them. Defeat had been certain with Lee in command. Now there was hope of advancing, or at least standing firm.

The young giant was a powerful force in combat. The American lines were able to hold and toward late afternoon, the British withdrew.

But not before a stray shot had found its mark. Peter was struck down the second time during the year, as both sides prepared to leave the field. Many months were to pass before he could return to action in another battle front in the north.

Monmouth was an indecisive draw. Clinton preserved his wagon train and moved safely to New York, though he left many casualties behind. Lee was later found guilty of disobeying orders and of retreating unnecessarily, and in time was dismissed from the service.

Finally recovered, Peter joined his unit at West Point in New York where Washington's main army was camped at a heavily fortified promontory of rock which jutted into the Hudson River. The men had drilled and marched daily while waiting for their next encounter with the British.

One week in July, 1779, Peter was ordered to report to command headquarters. In terse words he was told of a daring assault plan devised by Washington and Wayne for an attack on Stony Point on the west bank of the Hudson

River.

"Private Francisco, you have been selected as one of the picked men who will participate in a dangerous maneuver," said a staff officer grimly. "Your column will be led by Lieutenant James Gibbons. Other officers will command similar squads of picked men, striking the enemy from left and right columns. A third will march east along a causeway and force the entrance with loaded muskets. Most of you will force your way in with bayonets."

"Yes, sir. I'm ready, sir."

"The route will take you along secluded trails through the low-lying marshes. The water is high, so be prepared for deep, treacherous bogs that will slow progress. Your biggest job may be to break through lines of abatis the British have strung along the trails. Fallen trees pointing in every direction are part of their protective fortification from attack."

"We'll need skilled axmen, sir. I'm pretty handy with the blade myself."

"Good. We'll need axmen to head each column and slash the barricades. We plan to attack around midnight. If we surprise the enemy the garrison's ours."

The march through hip-deep muck and the abatises of fallen trees was almost impenetrable. Peter and Gibbons ploughed through perilously, leading the axmen in their column, while another unit advanced on the garrison from another level.

Wild shots zinged through the darkness. The sound of splintering wood echoed through the forest. The British fell back in confusion as the troops in the left-hand column stormed forward like a suicide squad. Before they could recover, axmen from Peter's unit broke through, Lieutenant Gibbons first, followed closely by Peter.

"Make way, Redcoats," he shouted.

"Surrender your arms or die!" yelled Gibbons in turn.

The three columns drove into the bastion of the fort. During the brief but bloody battle, Peter grasped his side at a scissor-like pain. He had received his third wound, a nine inch gash in his abdomen, but he wielded his sword through the final moments of the assault before the British surrendered.

Then he fainted and knew nothing until he awakened in a makeshift hospital at Fishkill (sometimes called Fishkill-on-the-Hudson) where he had been taken to recuperate.

Friends brought him up-to-date on the Stony Point venture. It had been a success, perhaps one of the most brilliant strategies of the war. Wayne and his followers, Peter among them, had slashed into the fort with such precision and speed, that the defending British forces were taken captive, wounded, or killed. In fact, Peter was told, Clinton's losses were so disasterous that he temporarily retreated to New York, delaying his move up the Hudson.

Another plus for the Americans was that the enterprising Wayne ordered the fort razed and valuable military stores and equipment were used by his own troops.

Now if the colonials could take Paulus Hook, the only important British post left in New Jersey, they would gain another advantage. Peter determined to be part of the maneuver. No mere bayonet wound could keep him down for long.

TIME OUT FOR HUNTING TOWER

Nor did it. Though not completely recovered, Peter disregarded doctor's orders a month later and helped attack the garrison with Major Henry ("Light-Horse Harry") Lee in command. The surprise attack, like that at Stony Point, proved the growing professionalism of at least segments of the American army. They captured a hundred fifty prisoners and the military experience gained by the men gave them increasing confidence. And, once again, they were able to add to their sorely needed supplies and equipment.

Meanwhile, good news from other battlefields at far-flung points cheered the soldiers. The Western frontier had calmed after Clark's victories and Sullivan's expedition. The Spaniards had cleared the British posts on the lower Mississippi. Demands in the West Indies prompted Clinton to leave Newport, leaving New England at least temporarily free from his occupation.

In the South things were more dismal. Efforts to recover Savannah from the British had failed. Washington's forces were reduced because three-year enlistments beginning in 1777 had expired, while English strength was building up. Besides that, inflation had set in across the country and seriously affected the military effort. Officers resigned when they had to furnish their own clothes and buy their own food. With nothing left to send home, there was a rumbling of mutiny among the ranks.

By now Peter had served out his three year enlistment, and he was weary of the strain of battle. It was a treat to return to Virginia for a rest at Hunting Tower.

Judge Winston had aged visibly and was bitter about the conduct of the war. He seemed to have forgotten that in his younger days he had helped encourage America's entrance into combat with the British, along with other patriotic firebrands.

Mistress Winston greeted the returning hero with genuine affection and praised him for his widespread reputation as a soldier of valor. Some of the servants had remained loyally on the plantation, but others had gone off to serve alongside their white comrades. Black Alex had enlisted but had not been heard from since. The plantation showed signs of neglect and decline, but it was a welcome sight to Peter and he was grateful for the warmth with which he was received.

Then the rain started, and continued at daily intervals for almost a week. The novelty of freedom soon palled and conversations with the Judge lagged. Peter began to miss his army friends and the orderly routine of camp life mixed with excitement. He found himself wishing for distraction to ease his inner restlessness.

He found it one day during a lull in the rainy period while tramping through familiar country in the direction of Willis River. Shouts from the post road hastened his pace and he headed in that direction.

A farmer, Alvin Smith, was frantically urging his team of six mules to pull a heavily loaded tobacco wagon from the deep mire which bordered the road.

"Slid off the main track here awhile ago," Alvin complained. "Now it's mudded in so deep, these confounded animals can't pull 'er out." He kicked despairingly at one of the wagon wheels projecting from the mud alongside the road. "That load yonder is my main money crop of the season. I'm downright beside myself with worry."

"Unhitch the mules," Peter suggested after a careful look at the position of the wagon and the tobacco cargo which was still well above the mire. "I may be able to give you a hand. Anyway, I'm willing to make a try."

The farmer looked dubious, but followed directions Peter tore off his jacket, pushed up his trouser legs, and waded in bootless.

Then, thrusting his huge shoulders against the rear of the tobacco wagon, he pushed and rammed with every ounce of his ox-like weight and strength. It budged. An inch, then two. An entire foot. Finally, with a mighty heave, he was able to move, half lift the wagon free of the muck and edge it to more solid ground.

The farmer was incredulous. "I don't believe my eyes. You did what six mules couldn't."

"Let's hitch up those animals of yours and see how they do now," Peter answered with a grin. "I'd hate to see a man's tobacco crop meet its end in the swamp."

"I'm much beholding to you, Peter," the farmer remarked as he was ready to drive off. "I've heard all kinds of tales about you being the Virginia Giant and a Samson-man in Washington's army. Now I've seen you in action for myself."

During the war years Peter's reputation had indeed grown until it became almost legendary, especially in Buckingham and surrounding counties. Stories of his prowess were woven around his amazing strength, his fury against the enemy in battle, his fondness for practical jokes. Sometimes he came close to causing hard feelings in his pursuit of pleasure, and his weakness for free spending and acquiring debts made him the butt of criticism.

However, most of his fun-loving tricks were tolerated by his friends who sometimes joined him in his wily deceptions.

One day he and Tony Debrell and a Buckingham friend, Mark Floyd, wandered past the old Miller farm near Curdsville where they spotted crocks of fresh milk cooling in a water trough in the farmer's springhouse. The rain had since halted, leaving blistering, humid heat in its stead.

"I'd give a pretty penny for a drink of that cow juice yonder," Peter said, glancing sideways at his companions. "What about y'all?"

"It would taste right good," Tony Debrell agreed, wiping sweat from his forehead. "I don't know when I've been so dry."

"That farmer believes in keeping his milk safe," Mark Floyd put in. "He has a padlock on the springhouse door."

Peter was growing thirstier by the minute. His friends joined him at the rear of the springhouse. He anchored his fingers under the framework of the slate roof.

"What'd say I lift this building at one corner and you two crawl under and set out two crocks of milk. We'll divide it among us and have a liquid feast."

Tony and Mark agreed. At the count of three he hoisted the springhouse frame high enough for the soldiers to shimmy under. He waited until they were inside before he let the building drop down.

They were trapped. Laughing uproariously at their surprised faces, he raced to the adjoining farm house.

"Come quick!" he shouted to farmer Miller, with whom he was acquainted. "Thieves are in your springhouse ready to steal your milk."

Alarmed, the farmer ran with him to the springhouse. Peter tried to hide his guffaws of laughter.

"You'll land in the brig for this!" Farmer Miller threatened. "A man's milk isn't safe even in broad daylight. Y'all ought to be ashamed of yourselves. Except for Peter here I'd be out of pocket."

Tony glared at Peter. "We're innocent. The guilty one is Samson there with the big grin on his face."

Farmer Miller stared at Peter, then back at the trapped men. "What's going on here anyway? How in tarnation did you get yourselves trapped in there? Any fool can see the door's locked up tight."

Still laughing, Peter ambled over to the springhouse and laid a hand on Farmer Miller's shoulder. "I guess it's time to tell the truth. I was just playing a little joke on my friends. It's gone far enough, I can see that."

He eased his fingers under the roof, heaved upward, and lifted the corner of the building from its moorings. Tony and Mark crawled out, stretched their cramped bodies and stared with disgust at their giant friend.

"You both have a right to be sore at me," Peter admitted apologetically. "But it seemed like too good a chance to miss. Even in wartime a body has to have some fun."

"Yeh. Fun for you," Tony said sarcastically. "But you've got this good farmer angry with both of us and no milk in the bargain for thirsty soldiers."

Suddenly to their relief, Farmer Miller broke into a laugh, and the three friends roared with him. To show there were no hard feelings, he invited them to a noon-time dinner of black-eyed peas, greens cooked with ham hock, corn fritters and fresh-baked cherry cobbler. And with plenty of cool milk to drink on the side. Afterwards they rested under the giant mulberry trees in the back yard, and in a happy mood, talked of their boyhoods in the days before the endless war.

During his brief holiday, Peter did what chores he could, but restlessness urged him back to action. Judge Winston had other ideas.

"If only you could stay with us longer," the old man

pleaded one day. Peter had been wandering listlessly near the deserted blacksmith forge, thinking of his old friend, Black Alex. "It's been a long time since we've seen you and you've need of good food and decent clothes."

"You're right there," Peter admitted, looking at his worn breeches and what was left of his undersized army tunic. His shoes had long since fallen apart and he had traveled home barefoot.

"But I must go back. And soon. Men are needed more desperately than ever."

"Aye, you're right," the Judge sighed. "But, remember, you always have a home here." He looked appraisingly at his ward. Peter seemed even taller than when he had entered the war, and was broader and hardier.

"We have to round up some worthy clothes for you, Peter. You're an important man now. We've heard how you're recognized by the Commander-in-Chief himself and that foreigner Lafayette and . . . ."

Peter laughed. "Tales do fly, don't they? I've been lucky in many ways. Certainly no man could have finer friends among the high or the low."

From Judge Winston Peter learned the latest account of Patrick Henry's activities. While serving three years as the first governor of Virginia he had commissioned George Rogers Clark to enlist recruits for the western campaign. Tales of their hardship, daring and accomplishments were a popular subject of conversation in the colonies. Most people were pleased about the territory they captured and the friendships they formed with the French and Indians in the territory.

Sometimes Peter and Judge Winston talked on long after Mistress Winston had retired.

"Thomas Jefferson's working for religious rights and

freedom in Virginia and elsewhere, but there's a lot of opposition. It takes a strong man to serve the public these days."

"Strong men are needed everywhere. That's one of the things I've learned these past years. The country's held back by much in politics and the war is overlong. Supplies grow shorter every day and manpower scarcer." Peter laid a hand on the Judge's shoulder. "I must go back soon. Next week, in fact."

Before he left, Mistress Winston oversaw the preparation of new clothes for the young giant and stout boots were custom-made to fit his over-sized feet. In addition, Judge Winston gave him a handsome new horse to replace Strawberry who had disappeared at Brandywine.

"At least now you can ride back in style," said the Judge with tears beginning in his eyes. "I pray this mount will bring you safely home again."

"Thank you, sir," Peter answered, touched. He's a fine horse and bound to bring me luck."

THE VIRGINIA GIANT SCORES AT CAMDEN

When Peter could endure the idleness of the Buckingham
County estate no longer, he volunteered (without
re-enlisting) to serve in the militia regiment commanded by
Captain (later the rank of Colonel) William Mayo of
Powhatan County.

He rejoined an army that was disjointed and in upheaval.
Congress had decided that it could not rightly give the
Southern command to the German soldier of fortune Baron
de Kalb who had sailed to America with Lafayette in 1777
and had proved himself an able and willing patriot.

Disregarding other possible choices for the leadership of
the American army in the South, the politicians appointed
Horatio Gates, who had been victorious at Saratoga.

It was August and hot that summer of 1780. The army
marched in the direction of Camden, South Carolina where
Gates hoped to cut off Cornwallis' communications from
his Charleston base. The route he chose was thick with
Tories and Camden seemed a long way off. The
approximately 3,000 men he led were chronically underfed,
suffering from a variety of physical ills, and mentally, they
were unprepared for battle. The truth was, that few, if any,
respected their new leader in the South. The popular choice
had been Quartermaster General Nathanael Greene, with
whom many of them had fought previously. When Gates
was appointed instead, their already low morale dropped to
a darker low.

Foolishly Gates ordered a surprise attack against
Cornwallis to begin the night of August 15 around 10
o'clock. His plan was opposed by his officers. They tried to

dissuade him because of the difficulty of uniting and maneuvering the troops after dark, but Gates was determined to have his way.

Almost simultaneously, Cornwallis decided on the same stratagem. He ordered his veterans to march against Gates at approximately the same time.

The inevitable happened. The two forces collided on the road, followed by confused fighting in the darkness before Cornwallis had the good sense to withdraw and wait for morning.

De Kalb, Otho Williams, William Smallwood and others of his officers hoped Gates would see the wisdom of retreat, considering that Cornwallis had well over 2,000 experienced veterans in his ranks to combat the inferior Continentals.

He failed to do so. When the British struck at dawn, there was almost instant disaster. The British regulars drove through the center of the American left. The green, worn-out Americans had no chance and knew it. Entire units fled in panic after the first charge.

But not all. Valiant men from Maryland and Delaware under the leadership of the physically powerful de Kalb held on the American right with only 600 men. They charged, reformed, and charged again until at last de Kalb fell dying from his eleventh wound that day.

In the meantime while men were fighting and dying, Gates looked out for his own welfare. He jumped onto a fast horse, leading the way to the rear in retreat. Then he kept on going, racing sixty miles away toward Charlotte, North Carolina, where he finally halted. Later, remnants of his defeated men struggled north and finally reached him at his temporary retreat.

Scene from Battle of Camden, with Francisco Part of the Action
Cornwallis Routed the American General Gates

(Virginia State Library)

However, another unit held firm for a time, refusing to retreat. Peter and other militiamen under Captain Mayo resisted attack after British attack. Tony Debrell was by his side, both temporarily sheltered by a convenient boulder that diverted gunfire. At the same time, they could make their own shots count.

As soldiers fled in terror from the battleground, Peter spied an unmanned cannon in an unsafe position in another part of the field. Britishers might take over its use at any moment when it was badly needed by their own men on the nearby flat.

He made a snap decision. "Cover me as best you can, Tony, I'm going to try to move that cannon over yonder."

"Hold on, Man! You can't move that thing. It's beyond mortal strength. I'll try to round up pull horses to do the job."

Peter sprang from behind the rock, crouching forward. He took a deep breath, leaned over and clasped his great arms around the piece of artillery.

Grunting, groaning, he straightened, then triumphantly hoisted the 1,100 pound cannon onto his back and shoulders. Slowly, painfully, he advanced, inch by inch, toward a cluster of open-mouthed soldiers.

Miraculously, no gunshot found its mark during the ordeal. Perhaps even the British who may have watched the feat were too dumbfounded! Gradually the young Hercules eased the cannon to the ground, gestured to the Americans to put it to use, before he half crawled to a nearby woodland to recoup from the ordeal.

Peter had no sooner recovered sufficiently to return to the battlefield when he again leapt into action. He had just retrieved his musket from behind the rock where he and Tony had been stationed, when he saw Captain Mayo trapped at gunpoint by a redcoat officer to his left. He

Peter Francisco Bayoneting a British Trooper. This incident is recorded in his petition. (Virginia State Library) — Photo courtesy McClure Printing Co.

lunged forward, killing the attacker, and saving his commander's life.

A few minutes later he, too, was charged by one of Tarleton's men. The trooper on horseback demanded his gun.

"It isn't loaded. It's harmless," groaned the exhausted Peter. "Here, take it." He thrust the weapon sideways toward the horseman.

The cavalryman reached warily for the weapon. At the same moment, Peter twisted it with a swift backward motion, reared forward with the bayonet tip and the British horseman toppled.

A quick glance at the now almost deserted battlefield assured Peter that the battle was over. The British had won an easy victory. Horseless, he saw his chance to escape capture. Nearby a British trooper's horse, without a rider, stomped in bewilderment.

Unhesitatingly, he leapt into the saddle. A clever ruse formed in his brain as Banastre Tarleton, Cornwallis' brilliant cavalry officer, and his men moved in to corner him with flashing bayonets.

Raising his body high in the stirrups of his "borrowed" horse, he galloped wildly across the field. At the same time, he waved his right arm triumphantly like a conquering hero.

"Huzza! Huzza, my brave boys! We've conquered the dam'd rebels," he shouted, pretending alliance with the British cavalrymen.

The enemy failed to pursue him immediately. Surprised by his quick, unexpected action and unable to indentify his costume at first sight as that of an American private, Tarleton lost his chance. By the time he and his followers realized they had been duped, Peter had spurred his "borrowed" horse into the dense surrounding woodlands.

Then, infuriated, they took to their own mounts, determined to track down the rebel who had dared pose as one of Tarleton's own. Peter escaped through forest trails, using cunning deception to turn off his pursuers. Finally, when he was certain he had left them far behind, he nudged the horse to a wide clearing where the riding was faster and easier. It led onto a quiet country lane.

He reined the horse in sharply at the sight of a figure trudging along the byway. The man limped along slowly, his body stooped with exhaustion.

The young giant halted abruptly. He had recognized Captain Mayo, his regimental commander.

"Captain Mayo, you're in danger here, sir. The enemy might find you at any moment," he warned. "And you look worn almost to death and in need of help."

"I have no horse. My mare went the way of many others, Private Francisco," Captain Mayo sighed. His voice reflected the fatigue and discouragement of his face. "Camden was an utter tragedy. When Gates deserted, most of the army did the same. A sad day for all of us."

"Yes, I know that, sir. And the British came on fast. If Gates had given orders to hold the field, things might have been different. A lot of the new men panicked."

"Thank God for those of you who fought back, Peter."

"We don't know any better," Peter said with a grin. He handed the reins of the British horse to Captain Mayo. "Here, take this mount and be off. An American officer is a special prize. The British would love to throw you in a brig."

"But. . .but what about you? I can't. . . ."

"Oh, they'd take me for a deserter and not such a welcome prisoner."

"But I can't take your horse. It's . . . ."

"He's not really mine," Peter chuckled. "You might say

Francisco putting Captain Mayo on his horse.
(He had taken the mount from a Redcoat.)

(Virginia State Library) — Photo courtesy McClure Printing Co.

he's on loan from the British cavalry."

Captain Mayo stared at Peter admiringly. "Now I understand why you've got such a reputation. Incidentally, word has already spread among the troops about your carrying that cannon. Why it must have weighed over a thousand pounds.

"It was a mite heavy," Peter admitted. "Almost dropped it on my big feet."

The sound of horses pounded in the distance. At Peter's insistence the officer fitted his feet in the saddle stirrups, mounted, and they said farewells.

"I'll never forget your kindness today, Private Francisco," Captain Mayo said with feeling. "And I give you my word, someday I'll repay you. Not only for saving my life, but now for this special kindness."

Peter plodded wearily back toward the American lines, arriving after nightfall. He was half-starved and so tired he ached.

That night he dreamed of Hunting Tower and the peaceful Virginia countryside of his boyhood.

When he awakened the next morning, he was still weary and depressed. He realized he was sick of war, hardship, and killing. It would be a blessing to be away from it all for awhile, and free. He had already fought long and hard, with battle scars to prove it. Men were leaving the ranks every day to return home and many refused to re-enlist or volunteer.

For a time at least he would do the same. The thought of life at Hunting Tower beckoned, and he started out on foot toward his beloved home.

Again the Winstons were overjoyed to see him. He soon learned all the late news. Black Alex was making a name for himself serving as a blacksmith with a division under Benjamin Lincoln. Several other servants had gone off to war and had not been heard from since.

Within a few days Peter was surprised to find himself growing restless. In his dreams Hunting Tower had seemed a haven from all trouble, but he had changed and so had life at the plantation. He was lonely and wanted to see old friends. Many of them were temporarily stationed at Prince Edward Court House which was a rendezvous point for militia troops from the Southside counties. Food supplies for the army were collected and stored there, as well as Greene's heavy equipment and baggage trains. In addition, a laboratory for the manufacture of gunpowder and a magazine for storing military supplies made Prince Edward an important center.

Peter's reunion there with old acquaintances was an exciting time of celebration. Especially with John Overstreet who had been commissioned a major since their earlier army days together. Within the week he was to join General Stephens in Henrico County so they made the most of their time.

They fished, spent time at a bowling green and at a county fair. Despite the war, villagers welcomed any festivity and fairs were especially popular with everyone. Peter's enthusiasm infected John and they persuaded local belles to accompany them.

He reveled in the horse-trading and swapped worn pieces of artillery for new, including a saber with a keen cutting blade.

"Why waste time trading back and forth for battle equipment?" John Overstreet queried with a raised eyebrow. "You've been telling me you're going to retire from the army and go into some money-earning business instead. I'm confused."

"So am I," Peter admitted. "The truth is I can't seem to make up my mind about the future."

They had been talking quietly between themselves near the livestock corrals. Peter had almost forgotten Deronda, the dark-haired girl at his side. She slipped her hand in his, demanding attention and he remembered his manners. He exclaimed dutifully with her for a time over prize-winning canned goods, cakes, and other foods from country kitchens. Bold in battle, Peter was shy and self-conscious around girls. He would have preferred to run off to spend all his time with the horses, pigs, cattle and other livestock. Especially the horses. Tomorrow he could come back, either alone or with John, to look over the animals more carefully.

Deronda got more and more on his nerves, though he tried practicing a courtly manner. He thought her over-plump and giddy and was greatly relieved when an admirer caught her eye. She conveniently got lost in the crowd and Peter was free.

It was not until after the war was over that he was to find a girl who attracted his interest.

When one of the townsmen, Jed Lawson, shouted an announcement from the center of the fairgrounds, Peter was ready to join in the fun.

"We're ready for the greased pig contest! One and all come join in the chase. The prize is a kiss from one of our loveliest belles and a pair of silver shoe buckles besides."

Peter and John joined the mob of wildly chasing boys and men who leapt and shouted like Indians on the warpath once the pig was released. Laughing, they soon gave up and turned to other diversions, like trying to climb a greased pole. Peter's size and weight made him an unlikely winner and John fell to the ground after his second try. The winner was a small wiry Irishman who earned his keep as a steeplejack in Lunnenburg County.

Recreation helped push back thoughts of the war, but Peter knew that he must make a decision soon, one that would affect his present life — and future.

HERO AT SCOTCH LAKE

Peter's resolution to return to the war front was hastened by unwelcome news. Cornwallis held all of South Carolina in his grip. Next, the British might try to move into North Carolina, and after that, Virginia would be in line for invasion.

Peter joined a company of cavalry formed under Captain Thomas Watkins of Prince Edward County as a volunteer. His horse was one he had bought at the County Fair. He had named her Victory for luck.

George Washington had finally been empowered by Congress to select a new commander to take the place of Horatio Gates who had shown himself to be both cowardly and inadequate to lead the Southern Army. Washington had chosen Major General Nathanael Greene without hesitation, though Greene had some hesitation about accepting the command.

Fortunately for the future of the Continental Army, he put doubts and modesty aside, and on December 2, 1780, he took over Gates' command at Charlotte, North Carolina.

When the word of his appointment was repeated from camp to camp, from man to man, there was jubilation — and fresh hope. Hope, despite the misery and discouragement that had followed in the wake of Gates' weak generalship, the defeats, and the consequent wreckage of what remained of their dwindling supplies.

Once again Peter found himself reunited in camp with his friend, John Aiken, who had returned to the lines after his second gunshot wound. Tony Debrell had also joined the cavalry company and the three veterans spent many idle moments in conversation.

"For a general who managed to learn the most of his military tactics and knowledge from books, that Greene beats all," commented John. "Or so I'm told that's how he knows so much. That, and experience. Anyway, he puts his learning to good use, that's sure, and makes less blunders than most."

"You're right. And he holds the respect of the men," Peter added. "There's nothing big-headed about the general and if there's anyone can outsmart those Britishers, it's Nathanael Greene."

John's face hardened in the sputtering firelight. The three men were cleaning their muskets in readiness for the next encounter.

"There's no officer in this whole cockeyed army I'd rather serve with, but I'm worried just the same. We've hardly enough artillery of any kind to go around, not to mention gunpowder. And we all know far too well that rations are scarce to the point of starvation."

Tony, who had been quiet and thoughtful, spoke up. "About how many men do you figure the general can count on? What's your guess?"

"I'd say a little over 2,000 by rough count – and less than half fit for action," Peter answered. "Half of us are barefooted, our clothes are ragged and our camps filthy holes not fit for humankind."

"Our worst problem's those cursed British. Greene's got a lot of worries on his mind. Here he is, expected to face up to Cornwallis and his powerful army and at the same time get back control in the South," John speculated. "I hear tell he's planning guerrilla warfare to shake up Cornwallis and I'm for that."

"Me too," said Peter. "It's action we need, not rotting away in camp, trying to keep warm and to forget our empty bellies. The sooner we begin the raids the better."

Less than a week later, he got the action he asked for. At Scotch Lake, North Carolina, his cavalry troop came upon an encampment occupied by the British, and they began to plot and plan how they could best harass the enemy.

The Americans were at a serious disadvantage. The only way they could hope to make headway against the enemy was to gain a foothill and rout the enemy from their snug fortification.

From a sheltered rock Peter studied their position and tried to devise a plan. If only. . .an idea flashed in his agile mind. If a man were to work his way up the hillside, the overhanging turf would offer natural protection. He could then sneak close to the fort, complete his spying mission, and with luck return to camp without discovery.

The daring of his plan to reconnoiter made his heart pound wildly. His scouting mission would take the utmost secrecy. He decided to slip out of camp by a back trail while his comrades were busy exchanging steady fire with the enemy.

Yard by yard he advanced up the steep hillside until he reached the overhang of the crest. So far he'd been lucky and escaped discovery. He clung precariously to roots and trees to gain each new toe-hold. Again, he crawled on all fours, keeping below the protective grassy summit, but searching for an opening where he could hoist himself upward to spy.

Slithering toward a great rock to his right, he saw his chance. A cleft opened between two mounds of turf and an imbedded root offered a strong foot-hold to prevent his sliding backwards.

Slowly he elevated his head until his eyes were above the level of the cliff. Triumph was tempered by fear. If a harp-eyed redcoat spotted him he would face a quick end.

His eyes darted from left to right. Dead ahead in an open field lay the British encampment. A guard paced back and forth, facing away from the embankment. Using the rock as a stepping stone, Peter wormed his way upward and over the top.

He had made it to open ground. He broke into a run while swinging low to the ground, hoping to escape detection from sharpshooters in the vicinity.

Overpowering the guard in a quick strangle-hold, he leapt into the tent where rows of hogsheads containing precious supplies were stacked. If only he could capture at least one and make it back to the lines! What a bonanza such provisions would be to his comrades and what celebrating there would be in camp that evening.

Peter could not resist a try, though he knew the risks of discovery. He grasped one of the largest hogsheads, flung it on its side, and rolled it to the entrance of the tent.

Now came the test. If he was discovered, escape would be impossible. The greatest danger lay at the rim of the hill where he had clambered onto the rock and skirted the overhang. Would he be able to find that spot again and then maneuver the hogshead over without discovery — or without letting it slip from his grasp?

Dropping on all fours, he crouched behind the hogshead, nudging it forward. Hopefully, it would serve as a moveable armor, if need be.

He had almost reached the edge of the sugar loafed hill when the enemy spotted the mysteriously-moving hogshead. Firing began. Musket balls zinged. One grazed Peter's back.

Miraculously he found the rocky cleft in the overhang. He scrambled down, pulling the hogshead after him.

From then on he met each new hazard head-on. In the open stretches he squatted low behind the barrel. His body ached with the forced wiggling movement. At the steepest parts of the hilly trail, he lifted the hogshead onto his back to keep it from racing ahead and cracking on the rocks below.

To his relief Peter noticed that musket balls no longer whizzed by his head. He must be out of gun range and close to home base. Jubilant, he rolled the precious cargo into camp.

Cheering soldiers welcomed him back. "Peter Francisco's done it again! Hurrah for our side!" came the shouts.

The hogshead was torn open on the spot. It was better than Christmas Day as the ragged troops discovered it held many of the supplies they needed most.

Firing had halted temporarily. The British defenders were uncertain of their next move.

Laughter and celebration swept through the camp. Friends and strangers praised the hero of the day.

To Peter the daring risk had been worth it. Though a formidable enemy on the battlefield, he craved recognition and applause in everyday life.

As though he had not aroused enough excitement that day, Peter hatched another scheme before the afternoon was spent. During his reconnaissance of enemy territory, he had glimpsed a herd of horses grazing within sight of the British fort.

What an addition the British mounts would make to the sadly depleted American cavalry! He still had his horse, Victory, but many soldiers were horseless. If only he could chase across the open plain and. . . .

Peter made another of his impulsive, lightning decisions. Borrowing a whip from a friend cavalryman, he jumped on his mare and tore wildly across the field to the grove of trees where the animals were tethered. He leaned low in the saddle and, one of the few times in his life, used a whip to spur his steed to a faster pace.

Muskets cracked. Redcoats cursed and shouted. Mortar fire from the fort rang out. Peter prayed as much for his horse's safety as his own.

Shots sped closer. Peter cracked the whip again and again, shouting "Huzza! Huzza!" as he galloped toward the grazing horses.

Once there, he slashed their tethers with his bayonet, then wheeled Victory back and around. The horse obeyed orders as though in conspiracy with his plan. Shouting, shooting toward the sky, Peter stampeded the band of horses back toward the American camp.

The barrage of gunfire intensified, but like a charmed deliverer, Peter aback Victory arrived safely, amid the cheers and shouts of the incredulous soldiers who watched.

Every man in camp was exhilarated by the day's adventures. That evening they feasted on roast sides of beef they had salvaged earlier from the friendly farmers in the countryside.

It was a high point in their lives. Peter's daring had given all of them fresh courage — and hope for victories to come.

These latest feats fed the growing legend of the Samson of the Southern army. Stories of his prowess spread from colony to colony and he enjoyed the kind of fame reserved only for the few. Soldiers clustering around campfires for warmth and companionship would come up with one tale after another of his strength and puckish humor. "Did you hear what Peter Francisco did?" would invariably trigger a response and the hogshead incident became a favorite story.

For Peter, Scotch Lake was a prelude to the most hazardous battle of his war career, one that would insure his fame forever as Washington's one-man regiment.

COWPENS AND WASHINGTON'S GIFTS

Soon after taking over his command in December, 1781, Nathanael Greene made the decision to divide his forces rather than let them operate as a unit. Recognizing the value of harassing Cornwallis with raiders at a series of outposts, he decided to divide his army so that they could threaten and wage small battles on several fronts at once.

Rather than keep the legions of Lieutenant Colonel Henry "Light-Horse Harry" Lee with his army, he sent Lee south where he was to join the guerrilla leader, Francis Marion, in continued attacks on Cornwallis' supply depots. He moved the part of the army under his own command across the South Carolina border into the Cheraws, and the remainder, around 600 men in all, he put under the command of "Old Wagoner" Daniel Morgan who had been brought out of retirement, and finally given the over-due rank of Brigadier.

Greene's strategy turned out to be a brilliant one, despite criticism from various sources. He schemed that divided they could obtain food more easily than as a unit, and keep Cornwallis so occupied in defending his holdings that he couldn't afford to make a drive into North Carolina with the force of his powerful army.

His idea worked. Cornwallis dispatched his cavalry leader Tarleton with over a thousand men to track down Morgan. "Old Wagoner" used his experienced military instinct and tactics designed to surprise the enemy.

As a battleground, he selected a tract of land in the shadow of King's Mountain known as Cowpens, a place where drovers had often rested and grazed their cattle on the journey to market.

Just as Greene had divided the army, Morgan decided to split his forces. He stationed the militiia in the front line of battle. On the first of the low hills lying behind, he installed veterans of the Continental line. William Washington's cavalry was to keep concealed behind the second of the hills to the rear.

Peter was worried. Though he liked and respected Daniel Morgan, as did most of the men, he thought the choice of battlefields strategically dangerous. The Broad River, around five miles away, ran deep and cold on that January day, and there would be escape for men who might have no choice but retreat.

He secretly hoped Morgan knew what he was about, that his judgment was as sound as his reputation for cunning, and that as a sly campaigner he could outguess the foe. Tarleton, who had tracked them down, was brilliantly capable of leading his crack cavalry troops in any encounter.

That evening before the battle, the arthritic-ridden Morgan hobbled about from one group to another trying to build morale, like a solicitous rooster. At the same time, he repeated the plan of battle. The militia under Pickens was ordered to fire two volleys, and make certain to single out British officers first.

"Look for the epaulets!" he reminded them. "Pick off the epaulets!" After firing the two volleys, the militia was to break rank and fall back behind the Continentals on the first hill, as though in retreat.

Tarleton did just what Morgan had expected when the British opened fire the next morning, January 17, 1781. With helmet plumes flying, his troopers changed directly into the gunfire of militia and riflemen. The British dragoons fell back, shocked, many an officer downed just as Morgan had ordered.

Hard, desperate, hand-to-hand fighting followed when Tarleton charged forward again with his remaining forces. This time he was cracked back by the well-trained battlers from Delaware and Maryland commanded by able John Eager Howard.

Peter, stationed with Washington's cavalry behind the second hill, could hear Daniel Morgan roar orders above the crash of battle. Howard and his veteran Continentals plunged down the hill, broke Tarleton's second charge, and the battlefield was a confusion.

When Pickens reunited his militia, reinforced by the Delawares, and swept around the first hill to strike the enemy from the side and rear, Washington ordered his cavalry to advance, Peter among them. They smashed around the opposite side of the hill, charged into the British right rear.

Just as the wily Morgan had hoped, Tarleton and his dragoons were trapped. The Americans had out-thought, out-fought a master of strategy at his own game.

"The Butcher," Tarleton, as the Americans often called him, was furious. He tried to recover his advantage, but William Washington himself rushed forward with his men and fought a saber duel with the redcoat cavalry leader. Tarleton was defeated and raced away. His dragoons tossed aside their arms and fled with him.

It was a brilliant victory, and was praised as the best-fought, most successful battle thus far in the long war. Hundreds of Britishers were taken prisoner and many others killed or wounded.

Cornwallis had another of his "nerve tantrums." The Americans were already over the Catawba River, too far away to be caught. The angry British commander took chase anyway, and to make faster time, he began to destroy baggage, including wagons, precious supplies and provisions. His aim was to beat Morgan and Greene to the Dan River and head them off before they reached Virginia shores.

Peter could scarcely move one foot forward after the other. His weariness knew no boundaries, and sometimes he had to halt from dizziness during the long march. They had eaten only one scant meal that day, and already many a seasoned soldier had dropped out, unable to keep pace in the effort to reach the Dan River before the British.

Winter sleet turned to snow and footing became treacherous as they broke fresh trails.

Nathanael Greene moved from unit to unit during the grueling chase. "I know you're worn out and miserable from cold and hunger," he encouraged the men. "But things will be better at the end of the march. We've got to keep going despite hardships."

"But we're down to the last rations," his storekeeper warned. "The men are sick and dying."

"I know that too well," said Greene. "But we've got to hold out until midnight. I've dispatched Colonel Carrington to salvage boats along the Dan, and I've pulled back General Lee from his raids along the Congaree with Marion."

"What happens if we don't make it?" asked one of his officers cynically.

"It means that O'Hara's troops which are heading Cornwallis' advance, could head us off. And as you know we're not equipped to fight and we can't open Virginia to the British," Greene answered with a trace of impatience. "Remember this, Cornwallis and his officers have their problems now too. Which gives us a better chance. They lost heavily at Cowpens, scouts tell me. He's already destroyed a lot of his baggage along the way, wagons and supplies, so they're going to run short on equipment."

"If it weren't for the dratted Tories adding to their numbers with men and supplies, the British might fare as bad as our own troops," one of his officers grumbled. "I'd like to see them raided out of the country once and for all."

"I agree with you. They're traitors all to our cause!" Greene glanced about, lowering his voice. "I have some ways in mind to ruffle Cornwallis' feathers. Guerrilla warfare is what he hates most, and it's what he's going to get more of — and soon."

The gamble to beat the British to the Dan River was a success. American soldiers safely crossed the river in the boats Greene had collected on the south bank. Cornwallis marched back to Hillsboro in disgust where he made a plea for food and reinforcements from loyal Tories.

True to his word, Greene kept the British nettled by raids on supply parties and leaders who might have been tempted to join forces with Cornwallis. Gradually, they ran scared, and fewer and fewer dared join the Loyalists. In the meantime, many of his men got the rest they deserved and food from the countryside.

Around March 1, the American general began to worry that the British might regain strength, so he ordered the army to move northward. Then for a period of two weeks he kept the men moving, but did not risk actual combat until the arrival of the reinforcements he expected from Virginia.

The new recruits for the army arrived on March 13 and 14. Though many were raw beginners without battle experience, he now had at least 4,000 under his command. Greene moved again, protected from attacks from Tarleton by the cavalries of William Washington and "Light-Horse Harry" Lee.

It was during this period that Peter was summoned to camp headquarters one afternoon.

"Orders from the top command. General Greene wants to see you, Private Francisco," an aide announced.

Peter was shocked. He reviewed his conduct over the past weeks. Had he been lax in the daily drills or in some camp duty? Was he to be reprimanded for neglect of duty?

Peter stood at attention. Nathanael Greene smiled broadly and motioned him forward.

"I have a present for you, Private Francisco," he said. "And I think you'll make good use of it." He turned to an aide who was fingering a long, oddly shaped parcel. "Bring it here, please."

"But who would be giving me a present?" Peter asked, mystified. He stared at the package in the general's hands. "And one of such size. Maybe there's been a mistake and it's meant for someone else."

Greene threw back his head and laughed aloud. "Not much chance of that. Few men in the entire army could use such a — well, Francisco, why don't you open it? Don't just stand there."

Peter fumbled at the cloth wrapping enclosing the package. Finally, after much untying, he stepped back, staring, hesitating to touch the shining blade before him.

"Aren't you going to try it out for size?" asked the General. "It was made to order special to fit the stature of the Virginia Giant."

Again General Greene motioned to his aide. "The letter, please, the one delivered with the package."

He handed an official-looking envelope to Peter who took it with shaking hands. "It's from no other than our Commander-in-Chief George Washington."

"I. . .I can't believe it. It's true I've long wished for such a sword in the back of my mind. But I never let myself hope to have one."

"The sword and letter were sent by special dispatch. The letter is addressed to me, but mainly concerns you, Private Francisco."

Peter's eyes moved from the polished brass hilt to the glittering steel blade. Holding it at arm's length, he tested its weight and balance. As Greene said, it seemed made to order.

He remembered an incident long past when he had jokingly remarked to Lafayette that his army sword was like a toy in his hands and wished for one that fitted his size.

"Perhaps one day you will get your wish, Peter," the Marquis had said. "It's true that the sword you carry into battle looks like a match stick in your hands."

Peter pointed the nearly five foot sword at an unseen adversary and practiced feint thrusts. "Those redcoats better look out now," he exulted. "It's the perfect size and the handsomest I've ever seen. General Washington has paid me a great honor."

"You're forgetting to read the letter, Private Francisco," General Greene reminded him. "It will explain Washington's reasons for having such a gift made and presented."

Peter turned a deep embarrassed red. "You've forgotten that I can't read, sir, ashamed as I am to admit it."

"Then I'll read it to you. The letter was written by one of Washington's secretaries and is dated March 13, 1781 from headquarters near New Windsor. It reads:

Dear General Greene:

Having promised to do something a long while ago about a suitable sword for one Peter Francisco, recently of the Tenth Virginia Regiment, who has earned for himself the honourable title of "One-Man Regiment," His Excellency, the Commander-in-Chief, has directed me to have delivered to you the sword which accompanies this letter.

This sword has been especially made as a testimony of his Excellency's regard and approbation of Private Peter Francisco's excellent and outstanding bravery.

General Greene smiled broadly at Peter. "He closes his letter with the words, 'It is a gift he richly deserves.'"

"I must find a way to thank General Washington," Peter said humbly. "Perhaps a letter with the help of a good penman. I will treasure the gift forever and use it in the cause of victory."

DOWNED AT GUILFORD COURT HOUSE

The March air was still cool, but Peter was grateful for the return of spring. Washington's unexpected generosity in giving him a broadsword to fit his size gave him fresh confidence and a sense of power.

Now that the reinforcements had increased his army to the strength of almost 4,000 men, Greene was ready for action.

While retreating to the Dan River he had selected an almost unknown site for his next engagement with the British. It was located near a brick building on a hill known as Guilford Courthouse, which was encircled by fields and woodlands.

On the morning of March 15, 1781, Nathanael Greene ordered his men into battle formation. Greene had been impressed by Daniel Morgan's brilliantly-planned battle lines at Cowpens, and with some advice now from the "Old Wagoner" who had left the army because of ill health, he drew up three lines for the battle of Guilford Courthouse.

He stationed the first two lines across the New Garden road, extending north and south. The third line followed the crest of a low hill north of the road. Each line was about 400 yards apart. Unfortunately the woodland areas created problems for the cavalry and also lessened the effectiveness of artillery. However, fields lying to the north and south of the New Garden road made a good battlefield.

Peter fought in a cavalry unit with the Third Regiment of Light Infantry led by Lt. Col. William Washington which anchored an end of the Continental third line. The two Virginia regiments which helped make up the line contained a good proportion of veterans in the ranks, as did the 1st and 2nd Maryland regiments which composed Greene's two small brigades of Continental troops.

The battle began when Lt. Col. Henry Lee advanced against the British near New Garden, a Quaker settlement. They pulled back, allowing the British to march toward the courthouse.

At the command to attack the British troops charged up the hill, confident of victory. Following Greene's instructions, two brigades of North Carolina militia in the first line let go with two volleys, then ran back and started to run. This was not surprising considering that almost all of the men in the brigades were inexperienced fighters without training. They were flanked by regulars on the left including Lee's Legion and Col. William Campbell's Riflemen, and on the right by a detachment of Lt. Col. William Washington's regular cavalry, a small regiment of Delaware Continentals and Col. Charles Lynch's Riflemen. Most of the latter had had field experience and many were staunch fighters when not hopelessly outnumbered.

When the brigades in the center of the first line gave way to seek safety in the nearby woods, panic followed in the second line. Part of the problem was that most of the men in the Virginia Militia which made up this line, were as unready for battle as those in the front. A few had had military seasoning and were led by Virginia officers who had fought in campaigns, but after making a stand for a period of time, they, too, retreated before the smooth-operating British attackers.

British guards led by O'Hara drove through both lines toward the top of the courthouse hill, capturing the artillery planted there. They were thrown back in a counter-movement by John Howard charging with his gallant Delaware and Maryland troops.

Finally, Peter knew that his time for retaliation was at hand. He waited for William Washington's command before cutting loose, a hellion on horseback, driving forward with his comrades in the only real cavalry charge of the battle. Wielding sabers through the broken ranks of the Guards, they swept into the tangled center of splintered redcoat ranks.

Peter was fighting alongside Washington when he slew two of the enemy. He paused briefly when his commander took time to praise him, even in the confusion of battle.

Applause from such a man as Washington pleased him mightily and drove him to fight harder and more skillfully.

He was at his best in the tangle of fighting that moved up and down and across the courthouse hill. Astride his trusted Victory, and equipped with his great broadsword, he was invincible. Horses dropped or survived on that history-laden hillside. Men screamed in agony — and anger.

Peter was one of the latter. Caught up in the frenzy of battle, his giant broadsword rose and fell. He was determined to outwit, outfight the enemy to the end, no matter what the cost.

In the midst of the terrible confusion, he saw Tony Debrell topple wounded from his horse. Swiftly he raced to his friend's side.

"Easy there, Tony. Try to breathe easy. I'll get you to a safe spot somehow."

He signaled a lone stretcher boy who was almost too frightened to move, shivering in bewilderment. The lad's helper had just fallen from a grapeshot wound. Tears swelled in his eyes.

"Ease him on gently," Peter instructed. "Then let's get him to the surgeon's tent."

Bayonets flashed. Shots rang out. Ignoring danger, the two carried Tony to a sheltered area where overworked doctors and their flustered aides struggled to care for the wounded.

Now Peter's fury on the battlefield rose to its highest pitch. He became the one-man regiment that Washington had referred to in his letter.

"Huzza! Huzza!" he shouted as he charged forward over and over. Then, in a sudden daring movement to strike down a British Guardsman, he rocked back in pain. His leg was pinned to a horse, thrust through with a bayonet.

The Guardsman hovering over him, Peter fought back the faintness, and despite the agony, aided the trooper in extricating the bayonet from the gaping wound. His attacker gestured as though to finish him off, hesitated, turned to swing back into action.

Free once more, Peter reacted in an incredible way. In a frenzy, he rushed back into battle after the trooper, ignoring suffering, ignoring the impulse to save himself.

Back in the lines he halted at the sound of a hoarse shout which rose above the sounds of battle. It was Cornwallis. In a fury at British reverses, he ordered his men to fire into the thickest crowd of men, British and American alike.

"Fire, gunmen! Fire, I say," he demanded.

His cavalry officer, O'Hara, heard the terrible order from a gully where he lay, wounded.

"Stop, stop!" O'Hara pleaded. "In the name of God, don't destroy your own men."

Cornwallis ignored O'Hara. His face was like grey stone. He ordered muskets fired into the mass in a senseless fury, destroying many of the enemy and his own soldiers.

Peter was dizzy and weak from loss of blood, but he fought on as the savage guns continued to explode and men from both sides dropped from wounds or exhaustion. Suddenly he was surrounded by eight menacing British

Guards. This time no ruse or superhuman strength could save him. He fell with his most serious wound of the war, a bayonet slash from hip to knee.

Cornwallis had given an order which may have been murderous, but it achieved its purpose. Nathanael Greene looked about, saw that all of his units were out of position and the lines thinned-out. If he had had any way of knowing that the British troops were equally shattered, he may not have sounded a retreat. But as always, Greene's first concern was to save the remains of his army.

Cornwallis was now in command of the ground surrounding Guilford. However, the technical victory he won was in some ways worse than defeat. He had taken some 1,900 men into action and had lost more than a quarter of them, either killed or wounded. His army was so weakened that it was in poor condition to renew the fight, while Greene's casualties had been comparatively few and his forces were still strong.

Cornwallis retreated to coastal Wilmington for new supplies and reinforcements. His departure left the rest of North Carolina open and Greene moved to Camden for the next campaign.

Peter would have been left to die on the battlefield where he fell had not comrades-in-arms saw that he still breathed when the smoke of gunpowder had cleared and the conflict ended toward evening. They carried him with four others of the more seriously wounded to a log cabin near the battlefield.

Providence intervened. A kind-hearted Quaker named Robinson, who lived in the vicinity of Guilford Courthouse, wandered through the deserted battlefield later that day. Fortunately, he stopped at the cabin.

Responding to the teachings of his religion to help his fellowman whenever possible, he examined the five men carefully for signs of life. Only one still breathed, though faintly. Without delay he managed to find Quaker Friends who helped carry the wounded soldier to his home.

It was there that Peter Francisco, close to death, began the long fight back to health. Only the gentle, loving care of members of the Quaker family during the nursing ordeal guaranteed his survival. That and the kind of superhuman strength that made the Virginia Giant an invincible Samson of the Revolution.

When Peter recovered sufficiently so that he could entertain visitors, he listened to accounts of the latest war news with the greatest interest, as well as to happenings in the colonies.

Word of his whereabouts gradually passed from friends to acquaintances, most of them soldiers.

One day he was surprised and pleased by a visit from Lt. Col. William Washington, who had seen him slashed down at Guilford Courthouse.

"How is the convalescent coming along?" he asked, staring at Peter's bulky bandages. "I hear you've had a bad time of it."

"My Quaker nurses complain that I don't stay still enough now that I've decided to live," Peter grinned. "But I'm doing fine, sir. In no time at all I'll be back in the fight. I hear that we've been giving Cornwallis a peck of trouble."

"Oh, we have him plenty worried all right. But unfortunately, the British flag still flies over Charleston and Savannah's ports are under fleet protection. We've lost some more battles since Guilford, but just the same, the

British seem to be losing their grip.

"Is it true that the war has moved to my home state?"

"Yes. It's a likely spot. It's well known as a training ground for troops and the British are after supply bases. Cornwallis has penetrated as far as Petersburg. Tarleton almost captured Governor Jefferson and some members of the Virginia Assembly sometime ago, but a militia captain, Jack Jouett, helped wreck his kidnapping plan."

"Hurrah for the Americans!" Peter exclaimed. "I'll bet there's an exciting story connected with that. I'll have to hear all of it sometime."

"You'll have some catching up to do all right." William Washington arose abruptly from his chair by Peter's bedside and withdrew a document from an inside pocket. "I had a special reason for coming here today in addition to my concern for your welfare. Private Francisco, I have a proposition to offer."

"Yes, sir. Go ahead and offer it. I'm curious."

"Many of our American officers and men have been impressed by your conduct in battle and your exemplary behavior as a private. Your exploits as a swordsman and cavalryman are widely known. In fact, you have a reputation for bravery, wit and skill throughout the colonies. A fitting reward is long overdue."

"But I expect nothing in return for my efforts," Peter said, trying to pull himself to a sitting position. "Helping best the British is reward enough."

William Washington's round, full face relaxed in a smile. "Spoken like a true soldier. But all the same, I'd like to offer you a commission as an officer. God knows you deserve a promotion if anyone does."

Peter did not answer immediately. He was surprised and pleased, but at the same time embarrassed.

"I thank you for the honor, Lt. Col. Washington," he

answered, after a long pause. "But I must refuse."

"Why in heaven's name?"

"Well, you see, I'd rather stay on in the fight as a private. It's hard to explain how I feel, but I don't have the education for a commission, for one thing, being unable to read and write. To speak plainly, I think I'll be better satisfied if I refuse such extra responsibilities."

"Francisco, you beat all I've ever seen. Any other man in your position would jump at the chance." Respect and admiration gleamed in Washington's eyes. "But I can see you mean what you say and I'll not force you."

"I hope you can understand my feelings."

Washington sighed and prepared to leave. "I do in part, but if you change your mind once you're out of that bed and back in the lines, will you promise to let me know?"

"That I will," Peter agreed smiling. "I'm hoping to get out of this bed and back to the action within a month or so."

"I hope you will." William Washington offered his hand in farewell. "If we had more men like you in the colonial army, the war may have been over a long time ago."

ENCOUNTER AT WARD'S TAVERN
AND WAR'S END

Still shaky and pale from his battle wounds, Peter began the long walk back to Hunting Tower in Buckingham County, well over a hundred miles distant. He missed his horse "Victory," downed in battle, both as a mount and as a companion on the journey.

The young hero stayed at Hunting Tower for an indefinite time. The big house was now occupied by various Winston kin. These included Sarah, the eldest daughter, unmarried, and a son, Anthony, Jr., and his wife.

After awhile Peter's inevitable restlessness returned. In July of 1781 he "equipped himself as a volunteer" and re-entered the army as a free lance scout to spy on the enemy. Troopers headed by the British raider Tarleton roamed from town to town to plunder, steal, burn. Horses belonging to the Rebels were considered special prizes of war. Storehouses of grain, other livestock or equipment were all in danger from the marauders.

Amelia County with its rich harvest stores was a particular target. It was in this area when Peter was on scouting duty one day in July that he had his next adventure. He had stopped at Ward's Tavern for food and drink, and upon leaving, found himself surrounded in the courtyard by nine troopers from Tarleton's Cavalry.

What to do? The dragoons menaced the lone American with saber points. All dismounted but one. Peter knew that this time instant escape was impossible. He would pretend to surrender, though it was against his nature.

One of the Britishers, the paymaster, confronted him, making a demand that riled him to action. Peter stared

Francisco at Ward's Tavern in Amelia County.
(Battling one of Tarlton's Troopers.)
(Virginia State Library) — Photo courtesy McClure Printing Co.

with contempt into the man's narrow, squinting eyes.

Looking Peter up and down, he noticed he was unarmed. A greedy sneer crept across his face.

"Give me your knee buckles!" he demanded. "And any other valuables you may have concealed under that tunic! Immediately, we'll have no stalling."

Peter thrust his right leg forward in a favorable position. "Take them off yourself, if you must," he answered with a hint of challenge.

The pig eyed paymaster was instantly furious. Defiance from an inferior — and an American — was not to be tolerated.

Tucking his saber beneath his armpit, the trooper bent down to rip the buckles from Peter's knee breeches.

Quick-thinking Peter saw his chance, rash as it was. He stepped backward, grasped the plunderer's saber by its hilt and swung it loose with a lightning wrench. Briefly in command, he downed his enemy with one swift blow on the head.

As the other guardsmen moved in for vengeance, Peter struck down two more, one of whom was astride his horse and had snapped his musket at him at short range. But missed! Peter grabbed the weapon.

At that moment the staccato pounding of horses' hoofs sounded from far off. Grew closer. Almost four hundred of Tarleton's regular cavalry were cantering toward the tavern from a side road.

Once again Peter resorted to trickery. His only chance to escape the remaining marauders in the courtyard was to try a ruse patterned after one he had used before at the battle of Camden.

"Huzza! Come on my brave boys," he shouted in a loud voice, as though to a waiting regiment of hundreds. "Now's your chance to trade a few blows! We'll soon dispatch these few and then attack the rest of the British."

The surviving troopers were seized with terror. Not waiting to investigate the Rebel's threat, they raced off to meet the approaching dragoons.

Peter had had experience before at "borrowing" enemy horses and herding them for his own purposes. Vaulting into the saddle of a white stallion, he drove all of the enemies' troopers before him except one. Just as Tarleton's Cavalry charged toward the tavern, Peter dashed down a half-hidden country road and into the woods, his booty of horses with him.

Tarleton was diverted from pursuit only briefly. He saw what was happening and on the spot offered a large reward for Peter's capture. In a fury at being tricked again by one of the enemy, he dispatched around 100 men to track him down.

The Virginia Giant was in home territory, and from reconnoitering expeditions, he knew his surroundings well. With his natural cunning he continued to drive the horses before him through a series of back roads and trails until his pursuers finally gave up toward nightfall. In disgust they headed back to their camp, knowing Tarleton would lash out in anger at their failure, but unwilling to chase an enemy who seemed to race in circles.

Peter had done just that. He camped that night near West Creek which adjoined Ben Ward's Tavern, only a short distance from the courtyard. The next day he again drove the horses through back trails to escape possible detection by Tarleton, finally arriving at Prince Edward Courthouse. There he sold all the horses but one and turned the money over to the army. The mount he was riding he decided to keep for himself. Ironically, he named him Tarleton after the British raider, and rode him in scouting expeditions during the remainder of the war.

Peter is said to have fought under Lafayette in some capacity at Yorktown and was there at the time of surrender when Cornwallis finally posted the capitulation document. Peter always remembered in later years the sight of a small, scarlet-clad British drummer boy standing alone on the parapet beating out the message of surrender on his drum. The request for parley was not recognized at first, but when the listeners caught its meaning, excitement broke through the crowd.

Shortly after an aide with flushed face reported to George Washington, who had been preparing letters to be dispatched to Williamsburg. Lafayette told Peter later that when Washington had broken the seal of the letter handed him by the aide his hands had trembled with emotion. The enclosed message which announced the news of a hard-fought victory for the American colonies was brief.

"I propose a cessation of hostilities for twenty-four hours," the note read, "and that two officers may be appointed by each side, to meet at Mr. Moore's house to settle terms for the surrender of the posts at York and Gloucester. I have the honor to be sir Your most obedient and most humble servant, Cornwallis."

It was almost impossible to believe that the war was actually over. The capitulation paper was signed that afternoon, dated October 19, 1781. General Charles O'Hara made the formal surrender of the British Guards on behalf of Cornwallis, and Washington asked General Benjamin Lincoln to receive O'Hara's sword.

Following proceedings, Washington and Rochambeau moved back north, and two years of waiting began. French and American commissioners met with the British in a series of peace discussions in Paris, seeming to take wasted months to come to final treaty agreements. Washington managed to keep a small army intact until April in 1783 when Congress ratified the treaty which gave full recognition of American independence.

For Peter it was time to go home. Before they left camp at Yorktown, he and Lafayette had a long talk.

"What I'd like more than anything, Old Friend, would be a good long visit with you at some place you might select," said Lafayette. "We've lost touch these last years and I've much to talk over with you."

"There's nothing I'd like better," Peter agreed. "I was planning to head toward Richmond to visit friends. Would that. . . ."

"Perfect. I have business there also and we can have a few days of rest and recreation."

Peter greatly anticipated his visit to the city. He had grown weary of war, tired of killing, of scant food and ragged clothes. When he got to Richmond he would buy a suit of the finest quality and sit down to meals that would outdo Mistress Winston's best efforts.

The sight of a young giant with his great sword swinging at his side striding beside the smartly uniformed Marquis de Lafayette created a stir on the city streets. People turned to stare. Girls especially.

Lafayette teasingly chided him for his shyness. "You're God's gift to women, Peter, and here you are, all of twenty-one years old and with no serious prospects. We'll have to do something about that, my friend."

"In time, in time," Peter agreed half-heartedly. "I don't rightly know how to treat a girl, Gilbert. You were married to your Adrianne at an early age and have her to go back to. You're lucky. I envy you."

The two friends were strolling leisurely past St. John's Church.

"You need experience and a chance to meet lots of pretty girls," Lafayette went on.

"If I just had more education and could read and write I wouldn't feel such a dolt."

Church-goers were beginning to descend the steps after the Sunday service. Suddenly Peter saw a young girl with blue eyes the color of the delphiniums that grew in Mistress Winston's garden. Her gown was pale blue with a tight bodice trimmed with lace. Loose yellow curls hung to her shoulders from beneath a matching bonnet.

By chance, or intent, she tripped as she reached the bottom of the flight of steps. Peter leapt forward to help her to her feet, getting his wish for a closer look at her face.

"Are you all right?" he asked. "Can I be of service?"

Dimples puckered the girl's flushed cheeks. "You've already been of help. I'm grateful to you, sir."

Peter watched the girl sweep across the street with a group of laughing friends. He turned to Lafayette who had been watching with amusement from the sidelines.

"There went my chance to become acquainted with the most beautiful girl I've ever seen, Gilbert. I've got to meet her again."

"I have a feeling you will," Lafayette answered, smiling broadly. "Promise me that you'll name one of your descendants for me, Peter, whether he have blue eyes like hers or black ones like yours."

"That I'll do," Peter agreed, "unless me she does deny."

Peter saw the girl a few nights later at a party for soldiers returning from Yorktown. It was given by the Carringtons at their handsome home across the road from St. John's Church. Her name was Susannah Anderson and she was from Cumberland County. Through inquiry Peter learned that she had been staying with the Carringtons to avoid the loneliness of her country home until her father and brothers returned from the army.

In time he also learned that there was a hindrance to a serious friendship with sixteen-year-old Susannah. A rival, George Carrington, was intent on courting her with marriage in mind.

Another obstacle was Susannah's father. He frowned upon her interest in an illiterate orphan with an uncertain future and questionable background.

Peter told Lafayette about his problems at a final rendezvous at Bell Tavern in Richmond before the Marquis departed for France. He felt at home and relaxed in the cheerful atmosphere surrounded by people and conversation on every side. He wished the evening could go on and on. . . .

"An idea just came to me," he announced impulsively as he sat with his friend. "What would you think about my going to work in a tavern, learning the business with an aim at advancement? Later maybe I could combine it with a small store and even a blacksmith shop on the side."

Lafayette was as enthusiastic as if the prospects were his own. "That's a splendid idea. Tavern tending's a respectable business and the store would serve all the gentry. You get along well with people. . ." He paused, his eyes twinkling. "That is, except for your shyness with the ladies. But that is easily cured with practice."

"You're jumping too far ahead of me, Gilbert," Peter laughed. "I have to learn the trade first and begin to save instead of spend. But in time it can all come true."

They raised their wine glasses in a toast. "I can see you as a prosperous merchant and Southern planter with fine clothes, carriages and a handsome family," Lafayette predicted. "Here's to the future of the Virginia Giant. May his every wish come true."

MARRIAGES AND COUNTRYLIFE

In the years that followed the war's end, Peter carried out his plans for self-improvement. His efforts were designed not only to please Susannah, but to try to win approval from the Anderson family.

Though it must have hurt his pride to do so, he attended a neighborhood school for a time which was run by a Mr. Frank McGraw. Peter was a quick learner and was soon able to read and write. In addition, he learned the rudiments of arithmetic and a smattering of the classics. He began to build a library of treasured books and became known as an interesting conversationalist on a wide range of subjects.

Despite his war wounds, his phenomenal physical strength appeared undiminished. Schoolmaster McGraw grew to admire his oversize pupil for his good humor and unusual traits of character. He had ability as a speaker, considerable charm, and a gentleness that was surprising in a former soldier of such formidable prowess and force on the battlefield.

Mr. McGraw once wrote about his pupil: "Francisco could take me in his right hand and pass me over the room, playing my head against the ceiling as though I had been a doll. My weight was one hundred and ninety pounds."

During these years he also learned the art of dressing, in addition to his scholarly accomplishments. No longer was he the rough-shod private of his war days. He loved to wear fine silk stockings, bright waistcoats, fashionable breeches, boots of quality, and for social occasions he was especially fond of high top hats to complete his outfits.

Susannah's father, James Anderson, died in 1782 and with this hurdle removed, he courted his blue-eyed belle during the next two years. George Carrington had reluctantly turned his attentions to other young ladies in the county, leaving a clear field for Peter. Finally, with the family's approval, the wedding date was set and in 1784 they were married in the Anderson home "The Mansion" in Cumberland County. Friends and relatives from the surrounding countryside were invited.

Peter wore a handsome tunic embroidered in silver and gold and Susannah's elaborate satin gown was the talk of the countryside. After a lavish supper, there were card games, dancing and other entertainment that lasted most of the evening. Peter was certain it was the happiest day of his life.

At the time of their marriage records show that the young giant was shoeing horses at Curdsville in Buckingham. A resident of the area at the time, Samuel Shepard, writes this about Peter in his diary in December, 1784:

"Joe took horses to shoe. I watched the blacksmith at his work and never before saw muscles as great and developed in so young a man. I usually write about a man's face. Of this smith I noticed first his great hands, long, broad, the fingers square, the thumbs heavy and larger in the nail than the usual great toe. His feet are as exceptional for length and thickness as is his whole body. His shoulders like some old statue. . .His jaw is long, heavy, the nose powerful. . .His eyes very friendly and kind."

The following year, for some reason Peter and Susannah moved to Charlotte County where he is thought to have built a house and where they lived for several years. It was during this time that two children were born to Susannah, a boy James and a girl Polly.

These must have been happy days. And busy as well. Tales of his prodigious strength continued to grow, and both the old and the new were retold to each new generation.

One concerned a carpenter named Tom Brady, hired by Peter to put slate shingles on a barn roof. His disgust with Brady's shoddy workmanship increased daily.

'You're not hatching the shingles down tight enough," he protested. "And you leave tools lying about. Be more careful in your work or get off my premises."

Tom Brady's temper matched Peter's own. He may have heard of Peter's war feats as a young Colossus, but if so, he was not to be intimidated.

"That I'll do – and gladly. Tom Brady's as good a carpenter as the next man, and I don't take kindly to your words."

Peter met his gaze. "I may use stronger ones. I don't like to see a man do a half-way job."

Tom Brady's temper erupted. He jumped from the roof, swung wildly at Peter, missed. Peter stepped back, clutching the middle-sized carpenter between powerful hands.

Tom shrieked with fright but it was too late. Peter grasped him by his shirt collar in one hand, and the bottom of his breeches in the other and heaved him into the air. He landed back on the barn roof where he clung precariously to a rafter.

Peter eyed him with amusement. The Irishman tried to collect his wits. He perched there jauntily, crowing like a bantam rooster.

"Well, maybe you can whip me, Francisco," he said, "but dratted if you can skeer me!"

Whether or not Tom ever finished the roof job is not known, but Peter may have admired the Irishman's sturdy courage and figured he had learned a lesson. His reputation for good humor and kindness to his neighbors, and especially the poor, became almost as well known as his feats of strength and his skill on the battlefield. His enemies were few, while his friendships extended from county to county.

In 1790 tragedy struck. Susannah died for reasons unknown, and Peter was left alone with two children to raise. It is fairly certain that servants, family and neighbors helped, but they would have been lonely years — and financially his income rarely matched his taste for luxuries.

Four years later his life brightened again when he married Catherine Fauntleroy Brooke in December of 1794 at her home "Farmer's Hall," which was located in Essex County. At various times he had land holdings in Cumberland County and in Prince Edward County where he kept an ordinary at one interval. Four children resulted from this marriage, two boys and two girls. One, born in 1801, they named after Peter to carry on his name.

In 1804 they moved to Buckingham and settled in a part of the county known as New Store where Peter operated a combination store-tavern.

One day in 1806 a man named Pamphlett pulled up to the establishment on his perspiring horse. Peter welcomed him as another prospective guest.

"Are you, sir, Peter Francisco?" the stranger asked.

"Yes, sir."

"Well I have rode from Kentucky to whip you for nothing."

Peter nodded, then called to a helper standing by and told him to go to the creek and bring him back a handful of willow switches.

Pamphlett, still astride his horse, must have wondered at the strange request, but awaited Peter's action.

When the servant put the willow switches in his hand,

Francisco Throws Pamphlett over a fence. The Kentucky challenger went home a wiser man. (Virginia State Library) — Photo courtesy McClure Printing Co.

Peter in turn passed them to his challenger, Pamphlett.

"Use these switches across my shoulders, sir. Then you can go back to Kentucky and say you've whipped me to save you further trouble."

Mr. Pamphlett was disappointed. He had heard tales of Peter's quickness to anger and readiness for a fight. The man was acting entirely out of character, he decided, and tried different tactics to see what would happen. He dismounted, and pushed his way through a gate leading to Catherine's flower garden.

Now he approached Peter again, asking to lift him up "to feel his weight," which was a customary preliminary in those days to hand to hand combat. Peter assented good naturedly.

"Now, Mr. Pamphlett, let me feel of yours," countered the young giant. Therewith, he raised the Kentuckian twice, then a third time, and then proceeded to pitch him over a railing four feet high and onto a road that ran close by.

Pamphlett scrambled to his feet and with a shamed face shuffled through the connecting gate. "Now if you'll throw my horse over the fence likewise, I'll go back home satisfied."

Without hesitation Peter did as Pamphlett suggested. After leading the horse to the post and railing, he thrust his left arm underneath the horse's middle and the right behind its rump. Then with a mighty heave the horse sailed over the fence as onlookers cheered and Pamphlett stared in amazement.

Following Peter's demonstration of strength, the man from Kentucky got back on his frightened horse and rode back home a wiser man.

Sometime during this period the Francisco family moved to Locust Grove where they lived an undetermined number of years. It is thought, however, that they lived considerably longer at this estate than at any other before or after.

While operating a tavern at New Store in Buckingham during these years Peter had every opportunity to make his plans come true, as he had outlined them to Lafayette years before. He made friends easily with all kinds of people and enjoyed the day-to-day excitement of serving and entertaining visitors who stopped by.

One day Colonel (formerly Captain) William Mayo, the officer he had saved from the British guard and to whom he had given his horse after the Battle of Camden, surprised him with a visit. He brought Peter a gift to honor his long-neglected promise to repay his rescuer for his bravery and generosity.

The weapon he presented was his favorite dress sword which he wore on formal occasions. He insisted that Peter accept it — which he did with gratitude. Some years later when Colonel Mayo died, it is said that he also willed Peter one thousand acres of prime Kentucky land. However, there is some evidence that Mayo's heirs opposed the settlement of the estate. Peace-loving when he had a choice, Peter did not contest the will and was never granted legal rights to the acreage.

During this same period, Peter received a second tribute from a former war officer and friend. One day a package addressed to him was delivered by a messenger on horseback. It contained a handsome razor case which was inscribed with the words: "Peter Francisco, New Store, Buckingham County, Virginia. A tribute from his comrade-in-arms, Nathanael Greene."

He was mightily pleased with the unexpected gift. For a time it carried his mind back to the days of Cowpens and Guilford Courthouse and other battles of the conflict. But not for long. His present life held all the variety and excitement a man could want.

Peter was well known for his high spirits and sense of humor. He enjoyed good food and ate lots of it, loved good fellowship and sociability. When in the mood, it is said that he could easily be coaxed to sing in a deep, melodious voice. One of his favorite songs was "The Battle of the Kegs" composed by Francis Hopkinson. He was a born storyteller, and spent hours talking about the past to friends of all ages — and color — and enjoyed a good laugh over tales of his exploits and escapades as thoroughly as his listeners. Probably something of a "show-off," he sometimes enjoyed entertaining guests by lifting middle-sized men, one in each hand, hoisting them to the ceiling with arms outstretched, as he had his schoolmaster Frank McGraw some years before.

He took pride in a stable of fine horses, especially his favored white ones. His love of fine clothes continued, and he reveled in parties at the homes of the landed gentry, and in turn, liked to entertain.

PAMPHLETT AND A NEW ROLE

At times when life in the country seemed slow-paced and unexciting, Peter and Catherine would travel to Richmond to visit friends or the theatre. One of their trips to the city in 1811 near Christmastime almost ended in disaster.

During a lengthy play which failed to hold Peter's interest, he became restless. The seats cramped his long legs and the air was stuffy.

He nudged Catherine and whispered. "I'm going out for some air. Want to come along?"

"No, I'll stay. Come back soon."

Peter had just started up the narrow aisle when he saw smoke drifting from a backstage exit. Almost at the same time others in the audience jumped to their feet. Flames licked from the stage. Screams of "Fire! Fire!" shrilled through the theatre.

Peter reached for Catherine, swung her above the stampeding people and carried her to safety in the outside lobby. "Go to the carriage quickly, please," he ordered. "I'm going back to help."

After Peter had rescued their friends, he returned again and again to carry others to safety. Some were so dazed with fright they had to be forced from the building. As in battle, the Virginia Giant seemed to be everywhere at once. His favorite waistcoat was torn, his breeches blackened and smoke scorched his face and hair. He is credited with rescuing more than thirty people before the fire was finally over.

Peter's great strength must have stayed with him even

Scene of the Richmond Theatre Fire of 1811. Francisco is credited with saving many lives.

(Virginia State Library)

past middle age. The story is told by one of his grandsons during a visit to Locust Grove, that one morning at breakfast his grandmother told of a problem with a newborn calf.

"Mr. Francisco, there is a new calf in a boggy place and the servants cannot get the cow to come away," she informed him.

Peter smiled his most pleasant smile. "Well, if nothing else will do her ladyship I will carry her out," he replied.

After breakfast the grandson accompanied his grandfather to the swamp. As reported, the cow and her calf were mired in, and though Peter coaxed and called, the stubborn cow refused to budge.

"All right, I'll bring you out," he shouted in anger. He tossed down some fence rails over the swampy spots. "Come on you old fool you."

Again his orders brought no response. Finally in disgust he waded in, tucked the cow under one arm, her legs dangling ridiculously. Then he anchored the calf under the other. With much sloshing and heaving, he was able to plant both the mother and her offspring on firm dry land.

It is not unlikely that once the episode was past, Peter would have sensed the humor of the situation and had a good chuckle. Then, together with his grandson, they may have broken into spasms of delighted laughter, unappreciated, of course, by the cow and her precious calf.

In 1821 sorrow struck again. After twenty-seven years of marriage, Catherine died and Peter was alone again except for his children and grandchildren, one of whom had been named Robert Lafayette Francisco to fulfill Peter's long-ago promise to his French friend.

He remained unmarried for three years, and then in

1823 he wed an aristocratic widow, Mary Beverly Grymes West who had come to America from England to live with her uncles Edmund Randolph and Phillip Ludwell Grymes in the Tidewater area. After marrying Robert West of Gloucester, she had moved with him to the western section of Buckingham County. She was widowed two years later, and then married Peter who was twice her age, but as far as is known, they were a congenial pair.

The year after his marriage to Mary, an important event brought fresh excitement into Peter's life. His wartime ally, Lafayette, came to America in 1824 for a visit. With an entourage which included his young son, George Washington Lafayette, the Marquis toured almost every large town and city in America.

Part of the time Peter traveled with him. Leaving Buckingham behind, he met the General in Yorktown. Knowing Peter's capacity for enjoyment and gregarious social activities, it is easy to imagine that some of the happiest moments of his life were spent in helping to show off parts of America to the visitors.

One of his sons, Dr. Benjamin M. Francisco, in a biographical sketch written in 1881, describes the reunion of the two friends with pride and sentiment:

"On his arrival at that place (Yorktown) he was invited under the marquce to see him (Lafayette). An aisle was formed for them to meet, where they made a most affecting and affectionate embrace. He escorted General Lafayette from Yorktown to Richmond, and from Richmond to Petersburg, where by request he was formally introduced to myself, brother (Dr. Peter Johnson Francisco) and two sisters, Mrs. Catherine Spotswood and Mrs. Edward Pescud."

Not long after his reunion with Lafayette, Peter and his wife Mary entered a very different phase of their lives when they moved to Richmond. A friend, Charles Yancey of Buckingham, nominated him for the position of sergeant-at-arms of the House of Delegates. In 1825 he was successfully elected to the position.

It has been suggested that Peter's third wife had wearied of country life and welcomed the opportunity to live in Richmond, which she may well have considered fashionable and agreeable to her tastes. Peter may have missed Buckingham, but he would have enjoyed the prestige of his position in the government and the associations with people.

They lived in Richmond during the last six years of his life. It was during this time that he was honored by a visit from Henry Clay, a former friend — or acquaintance. They had a get-together at Bell Tavern. Their conversation undoubtedly would have centered on the war, the state of the colonial government, and such.

Again his son writes:

"Mr. Henry Clay paid a visit to my father, I think in 1826. . .Mr. Clay examined his large muscular arms and asked if he had ever met with his equal. My father then told him that when he kept a tavern at New Store in Buckingham County, a Mr. Pamphlett rode up and made a full stop. . . ."

According to his son, Peter gave a full account of the entire story, and when he had finished his distinguished visitor shook his hand and laughed heartily. "I am glad to know that one of the mischievous Pamphlett family has been conquered," he said, alluding to mischievous pamphlets then in circulation against him.

Perhaps due in part to his traits of generosity and consideration for others, Peter was often in debt during intervals of his life. Of course, as has been said, his style of living bordered on that of a prosperous planter, and probably contributed to that indebtedness — and the law suits that sometimes resulted. His land holdings were never greatly impressive — not in excess of 550 acres in Cumberland County and approximately that at Locust Grove in Buckingham. He held land at various intervals at Dry Creek in Cumberland County, thought to be near the city of Farmville today; he had a residence in Charlotte County near Aspenwall; and as has been mentioned, in Prince Edward County; in Planters Town (Buckingham); and of course, Richmond during the last six years of his life. There may have been others, but nonetheless, Locust Hill is by far the best known and most closely associated with his ties to Buckingham as a native son.

Though it must have bothered Peter at times that the mystery of his abandonment in America remained unsolved, he never learned the true facts about his past.

During recent years research led one Francisco admirer and authority to the Azores where he spent five months. During that period Dr John E. Manahan of Charlottesville toured all nine islands in the chain. Finally in Angra, capital of Terceira (center for seafaring whale hunters), he found records of births between the years 1757 and 1762. With intensive searching, he discovered that a child Peter was born to natives of St. Anthony in Porto Judeu in July, 1760. He also found accounts of his sister, Angela, and some evidence that she, Peter, and several brothers were descended from Portuguese nobility.

Porto Judeu is populated by people of swarthy complexions and large statures such as Peter's and it is evident from findings that beautiful gardens and splendid homes existed in Porto Judeu two hundred years ago.

Dr. Manahan's research bore out that the child Peter or Pedro disappears from the records — no marriage and no death notice being found. He theorizes that the voyage to

Virginia being a long one, that if he were kidnapped as has been suspected, the sailors aboard the mystery ship abandoned him according to their own wills – perhaps rather than where they had been instructed.

One fascinating theory which has arisen about Peter's origin and mysterious abandonment on City Point shores is that his aristocratic parents may have had him abducted to save his life. According to this theory, Peter's father may have been a liberal of sorts in Portuguese political life at that time. It is suggested that he may have been found guilty of a political "crime" of some kind, perhaps differing with certain authorities, for which he was to be punished. In those days, according to at least one account, the penalty was a cruel one – the youngest son was beheaded as a retribution for his elder's "crime," if such it was.

This explanation (or suggestion) may offer a possible clue to the puzzle, though recognizing that it is totally without documentation, it might be well to think of it as a theory – and nothing more.

END OF THE TALE AND PLAUDITS
TO THE VIRGINIA GIANT

For many years after the end of the war (from 1784 onward), Peter tried to get reimbursement for some of his losses during the period of his service. Finally, he was repaid for one of his two horses which had fallen in combat. He was also awarded a small acreage in Ohio as an extra bounty and a very modest pension.

This, together with his salary from his position as sergeant-at-arms probably supplied enough for a comfortable living.

Peter Francisco, the Virginia Giant, died January 16, 1831, following an intestinal upset which today would probably be diagnosed as appendicitis.

Members of the House of Delegates eulogized his death, and as he had requested, he was granted full military honors at a state funeral which took place in the center hall of the House. The Episcopal Bishop of Virginia, the Right Reverend R.C. Moore, presided. The mourners were quietly assured by Bishop Moore that even though the dead hero had never professed a particular religion in life, he had "taken refuge in Christ" before his death.

Mr. Barbour, a member of the Virginia Assembly at the time, paid special tribute to Peter during the funeral service, calling him "no common man who was by nature endowed with extraordinary strength, the most determined intrepidity and the warmest patriotism.

"It was not his lot to be advanced in rank during our Revolutionary struggle — But as a private soldier he gave a striking example of bravery and performed exploits that have scarcely ever been excelled. . .Let us then perform due honors to the memory of Francisco. By the arms of such men the liberty of our country was achieved – an achievement of vast amount to the whole world."

The funeral procession led to Shockoe Cemetery not far from historic St. John's Church where he had once heard Patrick Henry deliver his stirring oration that included the famous line, "Give me liberty or give me death." In the procession were such notables as the Governor, members of the House of Delegates and State Senate, the Richmond Guard, and various other state and municipal officials. Salutes to the legendary soldier peeled out across the nearby hillside in final tribute.

Today in Buckingham County, efforts are being made to pay tribute to Peter Francisco. The Society of the Descendants of Peter Francisco, with the backing of the Buckingham County Board of Supervisors and the local Bicentennial Commission, hopes to raise funds to restore the declining Locust Grove. Appropriations have already been made toward the project.

In recent years the house became a Virginia Landmark and was listed on the National Register of Historic Places. Architect J. Everette Fauber, Jr., of Lynchburg, has made conjectural drawings for the restoration.

The Giant of Virginia has been honored and remembered in various ways. A memorial in Guilford Courthouse National Military Park stands in recognition of the part he played in that important battle.

In Hopewell (formerly City Point), Virginia, where Peter was abandoned on the dock in 1765, a bronze bust of the hero has been mounted on a granite shaft which stands in front of the Municipal Building on the main street of the town. It was commissioned by members of the James River Branch of the Association for the Preservation of Virginia Antiquities.

On March 25, 1975, a bicentennial stamp was issued in his honor and first released at Greensboro, North Carolina. Information on the back of the stamp reads: "Fighter Extraordinaire — Peter Francisco's strength and bravery made him a legend around campfires. He fought with distinction at Brandywine, Yorktown and Guilford Courthouse. He was a giant of a man and his feats were legendary. One of his trademarks was a five-foot broadsword. So great was his strength that he was said to have shouldered a cannon weighing more than 1,000 pounds. When he died years after the Revolution, Lafayette was notified and sent sympathy to Francisco's widow, remembering this man who had been a private in the army. . . . "

Just before the turn of the century, the Daughters of the American Revolution planted thirteen Liberty trees in San Francisco's Golden Gate Park. Each of the trees represents an original American colony and each is nourished by soil taken from the grave of a Revolutionary hero. Virginia's symbol was the chestnut, and in memory of Peter Francisco, the bag of earth at its base was taken from his burial spot.

At least three states, Virginia, Massachusetts and Rhode Island observe Peter Francisco Day each March 15 in recognition of his prowess in the Battle of Guilford Courthouse on that date in 1781 where he was supposed to have slain eleven of the enemy and almost lost his own life.

An engraving taken from James Taylor's oil painting depicting Peter's lone victory over "nine of Tarleton's Cavalry" at Ward's Tavern in Amelia County, is in the

A Bicentennial Stamp has been issued in Francisco's honor. In recognition of his contributions in war and peace. (United States Postal Service)

Virginia State Library in Richmond, Virginia. The engraving is inscribed: "This Representation of Peter Francisco's Gallant Action With Nine of Tarleton's Cavalry in Sight of a Troop of Four Hundred Men Took Place in Amelia County Virginia 1781."

A portrait of Peter Francisco hangs in the Governor's Mansion in Richmond. It is a copy of an 1828 portrait of Francisco painted by James Westfall Ford (signed) that hangs in a Louise County relative's home. The original portrait is owned by his descendants; the copy is owned by the Virginia State Library.

A documented sword is said to be on display at the Virginia Historical Society in Richmond, along with a miniature portrait of Peter (artist unknown). Colonel Mayo's dress sword decorates the wall in the office of the county circuit clerk in Buckingham Courthouse.

The razor case given to Francisco by General Nathanael Greene addressed to him at New Store in Buckingham County is displayed at Guilford Courthouse National Military Park in Greensboro, North Carolina (site of the memorial in his honor). The Greensboro Historical Museum has in its possession a shoe and other memorabilia.

In 1972 an area in Buckingham and Cumberland Counties in Virginia was designated the Peter Francisco Soil and Water Conservation District.

There is a Peter Francisco Square located in New Bedford, Massachusetts, which was a center of the whaling industry in America.

In Newark, New Jersey, a small park was named in his honor, and at Jennings Ordinary at West Creek near Crewe, Virginia, a monument stands in his memory. Undoubtedly there may be other ways the Virginia Giant's achievements have been recognized, but these are major and no omissions are intended.

Peter Francisco is a legendary example of a self-made man who earned the respect and love of men and women in high places as well as his friends and neighbors in the Old Dominion — and beyond. In these respects and others, he truly was a Giant.

The final paragraph of a short history about Peter written by his great-granddaughter perhaps best describes his legacy.

She wrote:

"Through low hanging boughs of Elms and Magnolias the winds chant soft dirges over his grave. The government cares for a soldier's grave, and lovers of history may pause to pay tribute to the memory of the man who fought and gave of his highest service to aid in winning the independence of the American Nation."